As Oth

Stories (

a

E

CW00502780

As Others See Us

ISBSN 9798853928350

Contents

As Others See Us

Jesse

I first met Alex at the track on a dark winter's night. Where else? We were both athletes in full training. Both running middle-distance. In the same training group, so we were bound to meet, weren't we?

Unlike me, Alex hadn't come through the age groups and development squads at our club. Alex was already a high standard senior in a different county before joining us. A good mover, I thought at our first session. Hard-working, focused, always hitting the target times, never dragging out the recovery intervals, always ready for the next repetition, never moaning. No banter during the session, but friendly afterwards. It was on that first post-session recovery jog that we got to talk, and we seemed to hit it off straightaway. Found out a bit about Alex's previous club and competitions, and how a job offer had led to relocation to our town. Talked about upcoming races and sessions. I offered to do a guided tour of local training routes. That's how we arranged to meet again.

So that was it for our first chat: running and work, no personal stuff. It was early days.

Alex

I first met Jesse at the track, of course. Two middle-distance runners in the same training group. Where else would we meet?

Jesse came through the age groups and development squads at the club and was now in the seniors. I was new to the club though, because I'd just moved into the area. I knew all about training hard. Yeah, I'd been through the ranks at my old club and had been following a schedule to get me to the National. Until I had to move down here, that is. So I needed to find a good club and a strong training group as soon as possible. And that's how I ended up training in the same group as Jesse, the day after I arrived. Hadn't even unpacked.

Couldn't help but notice Jesse at the front on nearly every repetition. Running hard, always ready for the next rep. Chatty, unlike me. I was too serious during training to be sociable, but with Jesse it was nonstop banter, taking the mickey out of training partners between reps, but also encouraging me. That was nice. Okay, I was experienced and focused, but it's not easy to move to a new town and walk into a new situation all on your own. Wondering what they would all think of me or if anyone would talk to me. It helped that I could keep up with them, but it was Jesse who really welcomed me. And then made me feel at ease during the post-session recovery jog, asked about the training I was doing before, chatted about races. And offered to show me the local running trails. So I knew we'd meet again soon. We seemed to get on well, although we didn't know much about each other then. It was early days.

Those days seem a long, long time ago now.

Jesse

That first run with Alex out on the trails was great. We ran at a relaxed pace so that we could chat. While I was pointing out local highlights—the canal bank for coasting along, the woods for speed-play, the quietest roads, fields ideal for long reps, the best hills for the really tough stuff—I was asking questions to get to know Alex better. Not being too intrusive, I thought, just trying to find out more about my new training partner. We were a good match, and even at that early stage it looked like we'd be running together more often. I was hoping it would be more than just running.

Alex wasn't giving much away though. Sure, I found out about the type of training advocated by a previous coach. And we both talked about the past season and our aspirations for the one coming up. I told Alex about my job, and my recent time at uni, where I studied English Literature. So had Alex. In fact we had the same favourite poet: Burns. Who'd have thought that two athletes running together up and down the rolling hills of the south would be reciting lines from *Tam O'Shanter* or *Address to a Haggis*? Or *Ae Fond Kiss*? Funny how that one came to mind. It's the way I felt at the time, but I didn't think that Alex felt the same. Seemed a bit cagey. But it was still early days. Like I say, I was trying not to be too pushy, but I really wanted us to get to know each other better.

Alex

I enjoyed that first run on the trails with Jesse. We ran longer than planned but there was so much to see. It was an ideal training environment, running freely along the canal bank and in the woods, and working hard on the country, especially up those hills. With the track nights too, I could see it all mapped out before me.

We were running at quite an easy pace so that I could savour the grand tour and try to remember where we'd been. It also gave us a chance to chat more and get to know each other. What were the chances that we'd have the same favourite poet: Rabbie Burns? Or that two athletes way down south would be quoting from *Yon Wild Mossy Mountains*, *Auld Lang Syne* or my personal favourite, *To a Louse*? Which isn't really about a louse of course, and Jesse must have known that and maybe read something into my choice but didn't say. Too polite? Maybe, but a bit too nosey about my job. But then again, maybe it was unfair of me to think that: it's natural to ask people where they work, and Jesse didn't mind when I asked the same sort of questions. No one would have guessed why I didn't want to talk about my personal life. Not that your job's all that personal, but I was worried about what the next question would be, and the one after that, and how much more I'd have to hide.

Which was a shame, because I liked running with Jesse and I hoped that we'd be friends, or, yeah, maybe more. But then I'd have to reveal things about myself. And I wasn't ready for that. It was still early days.

Running cross-country and the odd road race was okay but it was the thought of the track season at the end of winter that kept me going, although on those dark training nights it seemed a long way off. Alex felt the same but, unlike me, was actually winning cross-country races. As that winter dragged on and on, I saw more and more of Alex, but sometimes it felt like less and less. Sure, we were running together all the time but usually if you spend that much time with someone you know more about them, like their family, friends from the old place, and what they do when they're not training. But every time any of that came up in conversation, Alex would change the subject or clam up, and I'd feel guilty about asking. I wondered if it was obvious to everyone that I wanted more from Alex. They knew that we were training together between club nights. Did they suspect that we were becoming close?

Not close enough for me. Sometimes when a run finished outside Alex's shared house, we'd kiss (not just a peck on the cheek either). It seemed to me then that we both wanted more, but that *ae fond kiss* never led to anything and I was never invited in. There was a gentle hand on the chest, a subtle push away and a *see you at the next run*, and then I was on my own under the street lights, starting to shiver.

It was obvious to me that we were good together, and I thought Alex felt the same. Was it just shyness? Alex was a mystery, and I wished I could figure it out.

In more ways than one, I was frustrated.

Alex

It felt good to win cross-country races that winter, but it wasn't the real thing for me. The track season was what really counted, and I couldn't wait for it to start. Jesse felt the same way. But did we feel the same way about each other?

We ran together all the time. People must have wondered about us. I know that Jesse was wondering about me. Like, why didn't I say more about my home town, my family, my job? Why did our kisses never lead anywhere? I wanted them to, and so did Jesse; that much was obvious. So if we both wanted it, why didn't it happen? I knew, but Jesse couldn't work it out, and although nosey at times, was too polite to really press me. But as the winter dragged on and nothing more happened between us, I knew I was living on borrowed time. Sooner or later it would have to come out. I kept putting it off, but come the track season, Jesse would have to know.

It's funny, I thought again about *To a Louse* and why, of all the poems by Burns, that one always came to mind. It's the one with the line, *to see ourselves as others see us*. Burns wrote that it would be a gift if we knew how others saw us, because it would stop us from making mistakes in our lives. But I knew, from before, exactly how others saw me, what they thought about me. Jesse wasn't sure what to think, I could see that. For me the gift would be if Jesse could see me as I see myself, as I really am, and understand. Which is not what Burns was saying at all. But it's what I wanted. And yeah, I knew what Jesse wanted.

But I didn't think that either of us was ready for what the other wanted.

Not yet.

Jesse

The track season finally started and I was doing okay, but Alex was doing more than okay: winning, and winning well. So well that it was like the other runners were in a different race. Maybe they should have been. Alex was a different class, and really needed more challenging opposition. The times that Alex was hitting, there was no competition locally, not even regionally. It would have to be the UK Championships, and our club had a potential champion. Only the oldest club members could remember the last time that happened. This was history in the making. Everyone in our training group was excited for Alex, and we all wanted to do everything we could to help our prospective national champion. Especially me of course.

Inevitably, though, not everyone at the club was pleased for Alex. There were suspicions. To them, it seemed that the new star had come out of nowhere. Why the sudden improvement? Was it drugs? Who was Alex anyway?

I hated to admit it, but I was wondering too. But not so much about the running. Because, to me, it wasn't about the run. It was about Alex and me. If there even was an Alex and me. Our relationship, if that's what you called it, was still going nowhere. Call me old-fashioned, but wouldn't you have expected something by now? We were both consenting adults. But consenting to what? Training? Talking? Friendship?

I wanted more, and I couldn't understand why it wasn't happening. I'd been patient.

But for how much longer? These were no longer early days.

I wanted answers.

Alex

I'd been training harder than ever and running faster times with each race, even though I was out on my own. Winning easily was okay but I wanted more. And that would have to be the UK Championships. That's where I could really test myself. But where there would also be testing of a different sort. Yeah, I'd heard the rumours. I knew that some people at the club were searching on social media to try and find out about my past, although they'd never find anything, because I didn't use it. I had my reasons. Testing, however, would uncover the truth. Or would it? There are ways around these things. But could I take the risk? How much did I want to win? What if the truth came out? Where would that leave me? Where would it leave me and Jesse?

Jesse

The day of the UKs was finally here. I had just managed the qualifying time and was lucky to get an entry, but didn't get past the heats. No such problem for Alex though. Breezed into the final.

My own disappointment already behind me, I was there, supporting Alex. Watching them all line up at the start. All the stars. And our Alex, looking nervous. Not only nervous but scared. I'd never seen this in Alex before. Not in races anyway. Sure, I'd seen that look when we were kissing or when I was asking questions that didn't get answers. But never in a race. Was it because they'd all been easy wins so far, and this one probably wouldn't be? This was the UK Championship. Some of these athletes had been to the Olympics. Is that what was scaring Alex? Understandable. Was it too much, too soon?

The gun went and Alex settled into the pack. Moved to the leader's shoulder. Didn't look scared now. Supremely focused. Covered every move. Took the lead coming into the final straight. Stayed ahead. Just *ran away* from them all. Even the internationalists.

UK Champion!

I couldn't wait to hug Alex. What a race! What a star! But I'd have to wait, because of the standard post-race drug testing. A formality. Shouldn't be a problem for Alex. I'd been there at every session. Seen all the intense training. The rumours were just that:

rumours. I knew it was sheer hard work. Through rain, hail, snow, winds and occasional sunshine. Never missing a session. Always looking ahead. Never wavering. Ambitious. Driven. And now *this.*

Fucking UK Champion!

Alex

So there I was in the testing tent. UK Champion. I took the risk. I couldn't resist it. All that hard graft. Then those easy races. Had to test myself. And it worked: I won. But was it worth it? Now they were testing me. Well, it was done now. Decision made. I'd been ready to race. Worried, but ready. And now to face the consequences.

I was scared.

Jesse

Somehow I thought it would be different. A turning point. Alex was a long time with the testers, but it takes ages to do a wee after a race, you're so dehydrated. It would be worth the wait. I'd been patient. Hadn't wanted to do anything that might put Alex off as the big race approached. But it was over now. Unluckily for Alex, there were no major championships overseas that year, so there would be no international selection. This had been the final big race. Maybe we could both take a break. I'd been planning to ask if we could go on holiday together, but kept it quiet so as not to cause a distraction. Now it was time. Finally, these hugs and kisses would lead somewhere. And I'd get the answers I was looking for.

Was I being selfish? I didn't think so. I'd been the first to welcome Alex into the club, been a good training partner, supporter, friend. Would Alex have been a national champion without my help? Probably not.

I'd been polite, respectful. Surely Alex would open up now. And I'd get what I wanted at last.

Well, we both wanted it, didn't we?

Alex

My head was all over the place while Jesse and I hugged and kissed after I finally emerged from drug-testing. Was it my imagination or was Jesse more persistent than usual? Couldn't wait to suggest a holiday together. More than a suggestion. Sounded like it had been planned for ages. Was Jesse angry as well as disappointed and frustrated when I didn't give a straight answer? Turned away and muttered something like *as usual.*

And when I asked *what*, Jesse turned back and asked me to my face why I never answered properly, why I never revealed the real me.

Well, those weren't the exact words. The real me. But that's what was meant. It's all I could think about. Why didn't I tell Jesse there and then? It would be public knowledge soon. Yeah.

Jesse

I should have worked it out long before it came out. Looking back now, it was so obvious. It was conversations with friends that lifted the veil of denial that had hung between me and the truth for so long.

We were in the pub. Alex, me and a few others from the training group. Alex had been swamped with all the congratulations about the breakthrough win, and we had finally moved on to other athletics news. While the others were doing most of the talking, I was watching Alex, who looked exhausted. It could have been all the training and the euphoria of the win. Or it could have been our argument at the stadium after the race. Alex had been non-committal about the holiday, and then shocked and upset by my response. Every time I asked about something personal, Alex was always putting me off, as I had pointed out time and time again. When was I going to get a straight answer? There had been no answer to that question either, but we'd kind of made up and agreed to talk about it later.

We still hadn't talked.

The discussion in the pub had turned to training shoes, training, who else was running well and all the usual stuff like that. Until the conversation took on a more serious note when someone mentioned transgender athletes. World Athletics president Sebastian Coe had been in the news with his comment about *the integrity of women's sport* (being) *under threat* after a transgender swimmer had won a US swimming title. I'd seen photos of this swimmer and she did look like a man. I wasn't even sure what *transgender* meant to be honest. I assumed it was a woman who used to be a man. I could see how that would be unfair on the other competitors. I mean, this swimmer still had male hormones, right? And men are faster and stronger than women, of course. Some sports had already banned transgender athletes but at that time athletics was undecided. Then I remembered all the fuss years earlier about Caster Semenya (who also looked like a man), the best female 800 metres athlete in the world until she was told to either take drugs to reduce her high testosterone level or switch to shorter or longer events. Which didn't make sense to me. I mean, were the authorities *encouraging* drug use? And what difference did the distance make?

Anyway, by then I was so wrapped up in what the others were saying that I hardly noticed Alex shuffling towards the exit and making excuses about having to get home. I was still annoyed because of the lack of commitment and all, and as I said, we weren't really talking. So I didn't follow, but I did catch a look of distress as Alex glanced back from the door.

And then it hit me.

How could I have been so stupid?

That would explain everything. The easy wins. The evasiveness. The lack of commitment to our relationship.

Alex was one of them.

She was a man, or used to be a man, or was something in between.

My clubmates noticed my blank stares, and asked me what was up. Had I seen a ghost? Much worse than that, I thought and tried to say something but couldn't speak. Words stuck in my throat as I waved a clumsy goodbye and stumbled out into the dark street, where the evening chill collided with my beer-fuzzed head. Which I had to clear. Had to make sense of this bombshell.

But I still didn't follow Alex.

Instead, I shoved my face into my phone and searched for transgender and transsexual, which led me to gender-fluid, non-binary, bisexual and pansexual, and all that did was make me even more confused. Before that night and that look from Alex when leaving the pub, all I knew was *boy meets girl.* And now there were all these different genders and sexualities that I'd known nothing about, well not much anyway. I knew about Caster Semenya and the US swimmer, but it had nothing to do with me, had it? Except now it did. It was Alex. So which was she? Was she even a she? Was she a he? Or something else? And what did that make me? A red-blooded boy who'd fallen for … who? For what?

That night in bed I lay on my back, staring at the ceiling. Every so often I'd search on my phone again but it wasn't doing me any good because it only threw up more questions than answers. I tossed and turned and couldn't sleep. There was only one way to get the answers I'd been seeking for so long: I'd have to ask her. This time she'd have to give me a straight answer. Straight? Was she? What does *straight* even mean if you're not sure which gender you are? But does she? Know which gender she is? I didn't know any more. I didn't know who she was. But I had to find out. Too late to phone her, and her mobile would be switched off anyway. So it would have to be first thing in the morning.

I'd knock on the door and she'd have to let me in this time.

Finally, I'd get my answers.

Alex

I knew he'd come. As soon as I saw that look on his face as I left the pub, I knew. Concern, then shock, then puzzlement, all in a couple of seconds. I didn't think he'd come after me that night, but I knew what would happen next. He'd have to get out too. Have to try to make sense of what he'd just realised. He wouldn't understand. Everything was black and white with him. Okay, he'd been a great friend, training partner and supporter, and he cared about me, but he didn't really know me. And, like most men, he wanted more. I should know.

And then he'd realise that he had to see me. We had to talk. So yeah, I knew he was coming in the morning. And I knew I'd let him in this time.

But how far?

We didn't touch. We sat on opposite sides of the kitchen table, and he asked me. I knew, before he said a word, what he was going to ask. Was I a man or a woman? Which was I when I was born? He wouldn't ask me about sexual organs, male or female. He'd be too embarrassed or it would offend his masculinity and he wasn't ready for that. But he'd want to know. Then he'd ask about my sexuality, whether I was attracted to men or women or both.

He sat there, slouched, with his head down, not looking at me. He looked shattered. I could imagine the sort of night he'd had. Mine was much the same, dreading this confrontation but knowing it had to happen. He didn't look up when I started to explain. At first I stammered, and spoke in no more than a whisper. But when I saw that he wasn't going to blow up, and that he was listening and trying to understand, I told him. That, yeah, I was born a boy, but never felt comfortable in my body. He must have thought that was such a cliché but that's exactly how I had felt. Never wanted to play with an *Action Man* or kick about with the lads (but I did like to run), didn't like how they talked about girls. My parents didn't understand when I eventually told them, and my friends didn't know. When I was old enough, I started to transition from transgender (a mental state) to transsexual (physical).

He looked up at me briefly at this point. He'd probably learned from internet searches that there were different ways of transitioning. He was probably agonizing with himself about which method I'd chosen. How far had I gone? He looked at my T-shirt, and then down below. Immediately his stare returned to his own lap, and I knew exactly what he was wondering, what he wanted to know but couldn't bring himself to ask, and I couldn't bring myself to tell him.

And even though he still hadn't said anything, I knew how he felt about me then, which was different from how he felt about me before he realised that I wasn't who he thought I was. And that he wanted to know if I felt the same, or if I *still* felt the same, or if I had *ever* felt the same, or if it was actually possible for *someone like me* to feel the same. And even then, I couldn't give him a straight answer. I told him I was pansexual. Not homosexual or heterosexual or even bisexual. Because I understood that the gender spectrum is not black and white. It never was. And that it was okay to be attracted to someone, wherever they were on that spectrum. It was *normal.*

I wanted to tell him that I couldn't feel exactly the same as he felt or had felt, but that I was attracted to him, cared about him, and that we could make it work as long as we understood and respected each other, *loved* one another. And I should have said all that first before I tried to educate him about gender identity. I even said that athletics didn't understand the difference between transgender and transsexual, and that Lord Coe was no expert on anything to do with gender. That was the only time that Jesse sort of smiled. And even before I told him who I was and what I'd done, I should have told him how I had to leave home when my parents disowned me and then I had to leave town when my so-called friends found out and that's how I ended up here and that there was no job and that it was all about running away and that running was my escape and that I knew I had an unfair advantage because of the hormones and all that and I took the risk at the UKs because winning made me feel that I was worth something and not only that but that I was on top of everything and it was retribution but that the testing would find me out and it would be all out in the open soon and I'd have to run away again but that it could be an end to running in a different way if we faced it *together*.

But I didn't say any of that and I'd messed up because I was so fixed on explaining things without telling him how I really felt but it was too late because he hadn't understood and he didn't understand and he never would understand because we were so different and because of the look on his face as we finally made eye contact and what *was* that look?

And he *ran* to the door and I *ran* after him but I stopped at the gate and watched him disappear down the road.

Jesse

With a name like Jesse, you'd think I'd understand, wouldn't you? All that mickey-taking when I was at school. Then the bullying, the standing up for myself, fighting back, asserting myself as a good runner, winning respect. But what did I know about gender identity? My background probably made it *more* difficult for me to understand. I had to prove I wasn't a *jessie*. Had to affirm my masculinity, and I took that affirmation into adulthood.

So I was never going to understand, was I? No matter how I played the kind and supportive friend, I was always going to want more than *ae fond kiss*. One thing I'm beginning to understand is why she (or is it they?) chose *To a Louse*. Sure, it was cryptic but I think they were trying to tell me that they already knew how others saw them, or would see them if they didn't keep it hidden. And that they really wanted me to be different from the others and to look underneath the surface, to see them as they really are.

But I haven't done that yet, have I? *Seen* her as she really is.

I can't keep this to myself any longer. I'll have to tell someone.

Alex

He'll be back. I know he will. He hasn't got over the shock yet. He's still trying to work it all out. He still doesn't have all the answers.

Yeah, he'll be back.

And I'll be ready for him.

Jesse

I'm in the pub with Danny from our training group. I'm telling him that I'm not running tonight because I'm taking it easy after the UKs. So here we are, two mates having a chat over a pint or two, or several. Danny's asking me where she is. Knows this is one of the evenings when we usually run together. And I'm saying that they're not taking the night off and that they're still out there, pounding the roads. And Danny asks what do I mean by *they*? How many of them are they? And laughs.

And that's when I tell all. Everything. Right there in the pub, after my fourth or fifth pint. Slurring my words and feeling more and more offended and righteous and put upon and betrayed and lied to and hurt and confused and that I'd rather be here in the pub with a normal person like Danny than running with that *weirdo* who's out there right now and probably going to run right by this pub soon and I'm getting louder and louder and Danny is telling me to calm down and stop shouting because people are looking. And it's true. A bunch of yobbos are staring at me. How much have they heard? Oh, who cares? They're leaving anyway, dragging their knuckles along the floor as they lurch towards the same door that she used as her exit the other night. When she ran away. But then so did I, when she *told* me.

Oh fuck it, I don't care. And I turn my attention back to crying into my beer.

But it's no good. I'll have to go back to her. Not tonight. I'm too drunk. I've even forgotten Danny, sitting next to me, who's shaking my shoulders and asking me if I'm okay. Okay? I'm never going to be okay with this. Nothing's ever going to be okay again. Nothing's ever going to be *normal* again. She's tried to explain and I'm really trying to understand, but I still don't know everything. No matter how many questions I ask and no matter how many times she answers, I don't *know*. I have to *see*.

I'll go round in the morning.

See for myself.

Alex

He's here. And I let him in again. And we're in the kitchen again. And this time he kisses me and I kiss him back. And he shoves me against the fridge and he pushes his hand up my T-shirt and I flinch with pain but I let him. But he notices my pain and he stops and I say it's okay and I put my hand on his chest and gently push him away. And he looks confused again. He still wants it and he thinks I'm teasing him but I'm not. I've only pushed him away so that I've got space to do what I have to do next. And I tell him again that it's okay. I know what he wants. He has to *see.*

I have to show him myself.

I lift my T-shirt up and flinch again and he looks worried. And then he sees the bruises and asked me what happened and he looks so concerned. And I tell him about last night, when I was running by the pub to clear my head and those blokes jumped out and dragged me into an alley. And he asks me if they, you know, *did* anything to me. And I tell him no, they just kicked me around a bit to satisfy their moronic masculinity. And I tell him that it happened before. That's why I had to run away from the last place and come here hoping that, where nobody knew me, I could start again and everything would be okay. But it's not okay, is it? It's exactly the same. It's always going to be the same. And he's looking at me differently now. It's not concern or worry. It's something else. Is it guilt?

He lifts his hands up to his head and starts tearing at his hair and he staggers around the room. He turns towards the door but I tell him to stop.

Look.

And right there in front of the fridge, I pull my jeans down, step out of them and look him in the face. He's staring at me and I can't read his expression. It's not guilt. Is it anticipation? Desire? Wonder? Fear of the unknown?

I slip out of my underwear, and with a chilly blast from the fridge sending shivers down my spine, I'm naked, on display in front of him. I lower my eyes. Cold feet and wet knickers in a puddle of melting ice. Must have left the fridge door ajar. Too late now. I'm wide open, vulnerable, exposed.

I raise my eyes slowly, and his eyes are covered by his hands. He hasn't seen all of me yet.

I step forward and take his hands away, and his eyes are shut and I step back and stand there shivering, waiting.

He opens his eyes.

And, for the first time he *sees.*

His expression is different again. Not concern or guilt or anticipation or wonder or desire or fear of the unknown. This time I know exactly what it is.

It's *disgust.*

And he can't look at me any longer and he stumbles to the door and runs out.

And this time I let him go.

Jesse

What have I done?

It's my fault she was beaten up. Those morons heard me and they waited for her. I said she was a *weirdo*, for fuck's sake. She didn't deserve that. She was only out for a run, minding her own business. She shouldn't have been alone. I should have been running with her instead of feeling sorry for myself and shouting the odds in the pub. I should have been her protector instead of her betrayer. I'm as bad as those morons: I was manhandling her too. Okay, I stopped when I saw the bruises, but I didn't stop what happened next. How could I have put her through that humiliation? She was showing me what I'd wanted all along and what did I do? I just stood there. I should have comforted her, told her she didn't have to do this, it would be okay, everything *will* be okay. But I didn't do *anything*. I couldn't even look at first. And then, when I did, all I could think about was my own feelings. I couldn't handle it and I *ran away*.

But now I'm running *towards* her house. I've got to put this right. I'll forget the bullying about being a *jessie*, I'll tell her it was nothing compared with what she's going through, I realise that now. I'll tell her it's fine, *we'll* be fine. We were good together before and we'll be good together again. We'll accept and respect each other for who we really are. It doesn't matter what anyone else thinks about us. We'll face this together. She's not alone any more. It's *us* now.

So here I am at the door. She'll answer, we'll fall into each other's arms, I'll tell her how sorry I am, she'll forgive me, we'll tell each other it's okay, we've got each other.

I don't recognise the person who answers the door. It must be her housemate. But it's okay, she'll let me in to see her. She's probably resting. She'll know I'm coming. She'll feel the same way that I do.

The housemate tells me that she's not here. She left this morning, packed all her stuff and went, didn't say where she was going, it was all *so* sudden. Do I want to come in for a cup of tea?

No, I don't want a fucking cup of tea!

The housemate looks terrified and quickly shuts the door in my face.

And I'm standing there, on my own, in front of the closed door.

It's too late.

She's gone.

Run away again.

And I did nothing to stop her.

Fuck Rabbie Burns and his *ae fond kiss* and his *see oursels as ithers see us*. What did he know? What does Lord Coe know? What does anybody fucking know?

They're the only ones who know. And I can see now that it was as difficult for her to explain as it was for me to understand. But she tried, and I didn't. I let her down. She must have seen the disgust in my face. No wonder she ran away again. If I can't accept her for who she is, how can anyone else? She doesn't have to wait for the results of the drug tests to be told that she'll be excluded.

And now that I've finally realised that I love her for who she is, and fuck the *ithers*, it's too late.

So I turn away but as I start walking down the road, I hear the door creak open and I think it's her. She's been hiding in the house all the time. She hasn't left after all. Her housemate lied for her. She's been watching from upstairs. She's seen the hurt in my face and understands that I'm angry at myself, not at her. She'll run down the stairs and open the door and shout *come back*. We can be together. We can *do* this.

I look back, but it's not her. It's only the housemate opening the door a fraction and peering round, probably checking that I've gone and she doesn't have to call the police.

I stare at the house where for so long I was denied entry. Then I turn around again and carry on walking down the road.

Before I get to the end of the street, I'm running.

Perfect Patrick

Everything had to be perfect for Patrick.

Oh, how sick am I of that name. *Patrick this, Patrick that.* Even after all these years, it makes me want to throw up. *We need to talk about Patrick.* No we don't. Why do we still need to talk about Patrick? He's been gone *fifty years.* Fifty years, and I still can't get rid of Perfect Patrick.

It was great before Patrick came along and spoiled everything. Me and Mum and Dad lived in a tenement, which some people called a slum, but to us it was home and to me it was the best time of my life. The houses were built on two sides of a square, and the other sides were high walls enclosing a communal area with coal sheds, washing lines and a green, the best playground ever. It was safe too. The only way in or out was through a close, and as long as we obeyed the rule about not going out the other side of the close and onto the road, me and my pals could do what we liked. We played football, Japs n' British, tig, hide and seek; swapped bubble-gum cards and made up stories and plays. We were out all day long until we were hungry or got called in for a bath. Not a real bath, because none of the houses had an indoor toilet or bathroom. Instead of a bath there was this massive sink in front of the kitchen window facing out onto the green. Which meant that your pals who hadn't been called in would all stand outside staring up at the window and laughing at whoever's turn it was to have their weekly bath in the sink. Kids these days are indoors all the time with their faces stuck to a screen, but in the good old days we made our own entertainment.

When I was eleven, Patrick and his mum (my mum's best friend Jenny) moved into one of the posh houses at the end of our street. 'Our Johnny won't mind showing Patrick around, will you, Johnny?' asked my mum.

I say *asked* but really she was telling me that I didn't have any choice. I had to make friends with Patrick. I realise now that Mum wanted to show Jenny that I was *good enough* to play with the *golden boy*. That, even though we lived in a tenement and Dad didn't earn much money, we were as good as them. If I had known then what it was going to be like for the next *twelve years* of my life, I'd have said I was just going out to do something *really important*, so I was *too busy*. But Mum would never have believed me, because she knew fine well that I never had anything really important to do, even if she was trying to prove that we were equal to Jenny and Patrick. So I said 'Okay.'

That was all: *okay*. How was I to know that things were never going to be *okay* again?

That day when I was showing Patrick around, nothing was good enough for him. By that age me and my pals were allowed to venture beyond the close, and we got to know every inch of the neighbourhood. Patrick said that it must have been a relief to get away from all that *oppressiveness* (whatever that meant) and that *where he used to live* they had a big garden and *three* toilets, all *inside the house*. Anyway, I let that remark pass, which at the time I thought was *quite mature* of me, and showed Patrick the local slag heap where we used to climb up on our hands and knees, and slide back down on our backsides. We'd go home with black hands, black knees and black bums, which our mums would skelp hard, and then they'd shout at us and send us to bed without any dinner. The next day we'd have to run around in our underpants until our mucky clothes were clean and dry. As I said, we made our own entertainment in those days. It was *good enough* for us.

But not for Smarty Pants Patrick. Oh no, the dirty black slag heap wasn't anywhere *near* good enough for him. Because, *where he used to live* there was a *mountain* behind the house.

Him and his pals used to take a *ski lift* to the top and come back down the lovely clean white snow on a *toboggan*. No skelps on the bum for that lot. I didn't even know what a *toboggan* was, but I wasn't going to let Poncy Perfect know that, so I just smiled and nodded.

That's what it was like all day. After the slag heap I showed him the river and he went all snooty and said it was just an *elongated puddle*. *Where he used to live* the river was ten times as wide and they spent most of the summer rowing or kayaking. Did I know that their garden went all the way down to the riverside, where their friends always *berthed* their boats at his *private jetty* when they came round for *cocktails*? No, I didn't know that, but I kept my mouth shut, still being *quite mature*, you understand. Okay, I made that up about the cocktails, but Patrick was such a dickhead. I'd only spent a few hours with him and already I was wishing he'd never been *berthed* himself.

I could go on—like when he told me the shops *where he used to live* were five floors higher than ours, the football team was two divisions higher, they had a *beautiful, expansive* forest (we just climbed trees in the woods)—but you get the picture. And that was only the first day. Patrick, spelt P-R-I-C-K.

Anyway, if it was so great *where he used to live*, what was Patrick the Prick doing living round here now, even in one of the posh houses? No snow-capped mountains, free-flowing rivers, beautiful-expansive forests, multi-storey shops or top-notch football teams round here, pal. No poncy toboggans, jetties or kayaks either. If he was too perfect to get down and dirty with the rest of us scrabbling around the slag heap, why didn't he go back to his poncy-perfect home?

Being mature and all, I think I knew the answer. His dad had left home, and apparently Patrick's mum had had to *scale back* because *times were hard*. Mum hoped that Jenny had moved house so that she could be close to her loving friend's comfort and support. But that's one thing that I understood better than Mum did: Jenny didn't want any *comfort* or *support*. She only wanted to prove that they were still better than us, even although they had *fallen on hard times*. I also knew that, no matter how much she stuck her nose up in the air and pretended how *superior* she and Patrick were to us, she was really jealous of what we had. My dad was still around and always would be. And I had my pals, whereas Patrick had left his swanning up his precious river.

I reckon Patrick was jealous too. Why else would he copy everything I did and then outdo me? He said he didn't like the things I liked, but he did them anyway. For instance, a few days after disrespecting our slag heap and sneering at the black muck on us, he turned up in waterproof coat and trousers so that he wouldn't get his good clothes dirty. He actually joined in with us climbing up and sliding down on the slag.

That's when I found out what a toboggan is.

Which couldn't have come cheap. So much for *hard times*. In fact, I couldn't see any signs at all of *scaling back*. The truth is that Patrick was his mummy's shining boy, and his absent father made sure that the jewel in the family's crown never wanted for anything.

After the toboggan came Subbuteo table football. Except none of our mums had a table to spare, so me and my pals always rolled the cloth pitch out onto the carpet and contorted ourselves around the playing area, trying and failing not to stick the knee on top of one of the plastic players and break his legs.

'Boring!' declared Prim and Proper Patrick, but the following week he invited me round to his posh house to see his new custom-built table with corner flags, scoreboard, grandstands and a team painted especially in his old top-notch team's colours. If that wasn't enough, he beat me every time. Annoying!

When we were teenagers I got into punk, spiked my hair and wore drainpipe jeans with holes in them and a beat-up leather jacket. Not Preening Patrick. Oh no, he had his hair immaculately permed and got a fashionable trench coat that was so long it touched his perfect toes. Mum said it must have cost a fortune. Poor Mum, she couldn't see what I could see: that Posh Patrick was a snob who always had to be better than us, just like his mum. My mum still wanted me to be like Patrick. She didn't understand that me and Patrick were different. And so were Mum and Jenny, but Mum was still hanging on to the dream of Best Friends Forever.

Anyway, how did that trench coat even work? He wasn't going to roll around in any trench, was he? Even if he did, he'd be bound to trip over the stupid, poncy thing. He thought he was the height of fashion but he just looked like a prat. For a start, he was the only one with a perm. But it seemed to work with the girls. 'Oh, he's got such lovely hair, I wish I could get my hair looking like that,' they would say, and try to get off with him.

But Patrick the Preening Prat wasn't interested, and why would he have been? He'd already found his perfect partner: *himself*.

One of the great things about punk was that you and your pals could pick up a guitar, learn a few chords and shout about things that annoyed you. And the thing that annoyed me most was Patrick the Proper Prick. When I saved up all my Saturday job money and bought a cheap guitar, Patrick, true to form, sneered at it. According to him it wasn't *proper music*, it was just a racket and a lot of shouting, and we couldn't play our instruments and neither could the Clash, the Sex Pistols or the Damned. He just didn't get it, and I thought that would be the end of it. But no, not Want for Nothing Patrick. His mum bought him a guitar, drum kit *and* keyboards. Like I said, always had to outdo me.

When we left school I got a decent job in town. Not a brilliant job but a steady one, *good enough* for me. But as usual, Perfect Patrick looked down on me, because he was going to university so that he could improve his mind, get the perfect job and make a million. It was testing all my hard-won maturity to stop me from smashing his stuck-up perfect nose into his perfect face, but to keep Mum happy I *turned the other cheek*.

Mum was quite proud of me, actually. So was Dad, who was always a steady influence, grateful for what he had. And by his example, I was happy with what I had too, especially with my Annoying Nemesis out of the way at uni for a while. Mum and Dad were pleased that I seemed ready to settle down. Steady job, well-liked and respected locally (still had all my old pals, not like Lonely Boy Patrick) and a lovely girlfriend, Julie, with the honestly-blue eyes.

Years passed; I was doing well at work and going steady with Julie, and Patrick got his poncy degree. And this is where the jealous prick came into his own. Nowadays he would have chatted up a girl on social media but that wouldn't have been as spectacular as what Anything You Can Do I Can Do Better Patrick did then. He turned up at Julie's house, with his newly styled hair, a new trench coat (yes, another one), an enormous bunch of roses and *in a brand-new sports car*. And Julie fell for it. Not straight away—she wasn't *that* shallow—but Think of Everything Patrick gradually wore her down.

Up against that, I had no chance. There was no point in talking to Patrick about it. You couldn't reason with the prick. He was so far up his own arse that he would never listen. All he could think about was himself and how to outdo his underprivileged pal, who nevertheless had everything that he didn't: a dad who was always there, friends who stuck by me, a steady girlfriend (although not any more: I was dumped). Patrick the Perfect Prat probably didn't even like Julie that much. And she couldn't compete with his true love: *himself*.

By that time I'd had enough of *being mature*. This was the final insult. There was only one thing to do. I had to get rid of Poisonous Patrick. But how? Whatever it was, it had to make him go away forever.

I considered poison, actually. But how could I have got past his mum to put something in his food? And how would I know that his mum wouldn't eat it by accident? She wasn't my favourite person but I didn't wish any harm on her. I could have slipped something in his pint, but when he went to the pub it was always with Julie, and I wouldn't get past her either. Even if I did, they'd be snogging, so she'd pick up the poison from his lips and that would never do. I'd need her later.

I could have tried the old push-him-in-front-of-a-train trick, but he never took the train. Why would he, with his posh new sports car?

What about a hit man? Nowadays you could probably find something like *Assassins Anonymous* online. Back then you let your fingers do the walking and looked up *Yellow Pages*, and it was surprisingly easy to read through the lines if you really wanted to.

JEALOUS OF A POP STAR?
WANT TO MAKE A HIT?
NO JOB TOO SMALL.
CONTACT OUR STUDIO TODAY.
NO QUESTIONS ASKED.
CASH ONLY.
TERMS AND CONDITIONS APPLY.

But I had a feeling that it would hit my finances too hard, and I needed to save up for when I got Julie back and we settled down together.

What to do?

And then it came to me. Even though Patrick didn't like to do what I did, he always did it anyway. So, all I had to do was to let it be known what I was doing.

Something that he wasn't very good at but he'd have to do it so that he could do it better than I could.

Something dangerous.

Something that would get rid of him once and for all.

Something that would look like an accident.

That no one could blame me for.

It had to be the perfect crime to get rid of Perfect Patrick.

It would be a victimless crime.

Except for Poor Patrick of course.

But he was so perfect, he was bound to have a place in heaven.

And that made it okay.

*

Me and Julie are sitting in our usual chairs in the living room. The same chairs we've sat in for decades. Julie's watching a nature programme on TV and I'm reading the sports pages of the Sunday paper. Between our chairs are stacks of packing boxes. We've both been retired for a while now, and we've finally decided to *downsize*. In only a few days' time we'll be moving to that cottage in the country that I've been promising Julie for ages. After nearly fifty years of *wedded bliss*, we're going to see out our days together in *perfect peace*.

I say *bliss* and *perfect peace*, but we've had our arguments along the way. Who doesn't? Only last week, we disagreed about what to keep and what to get rid of, even after several trips to the charity shops and the recycling centre. I managed to salvage some of my old

Subbuteo players, the ones with their legs *not* broken, enough to make up a team, which I painted in our grandson's favourite team's colours. So we passed that on, but I wanted to keep my old guitar, which Julie doesn't believe is a collector's item. And there was not one but two trench coats, which Julie wanted to keep for *sentimental* reasons, but I wanted to chuck out for *obvious* reasons. So we compromised: I kept the guitar and she kept the coats.

Julie turns away from the TV for a change and peers at me over the top of the boxes. 'Johnny, *we need to talk about Patrick*.'

I'm thinking: *No we don't,* but I *say*: 'Why do we still need to talk about Patrick? He's been gone *fifty years*.' Fifty years, and I still can't get rid of That Prat Patrick. How sick am I of that name.

'There's no point in sticking your head in the paper like a giraffe,' she says.

'Ostrich.'

'What stitch? What are you talking about?'

'Turn the TV down and you might hear me. Not a *stitch*. An *ostrich*. It's ostriches that stick their heads in the sand. Giraffes stick them up trees.'

'Okay, you knew what I meant. You know I get mixed up these days.'

'But you've been watching one on TV for the last half an hour.'

'What?'

'An ostrich.'

'Oh, that thing.'

Sometimes it's hard to follow her gist. It must be dementia. Julie's, not mine.

'I might get confused sometimes but I never forget dates,' she says. I always copy them onto the calendar from the year before, when my memory was better, I think. Anyway, do you know what date's coming up?'

This could be a trick question. I know it's our wedding anniversary soon, but not that soon, and it'll be our forty-ninth, not the big one in a year's time. So, I don't answer—she'll tell me herself if she remembers—and I get back to the football scores. Hm, I see that our team won in the Premier League again, not like Poncy Patrick's so-called top-notch side, who've been in League One for ages.

'It'll be the fiftieth anniversary of Patrick's death soon,' she says. 'We should do something, like a memorial service.'

'What for? Why *us*?'

'Look, Johnny, I may forget things but I haven't forgotten that Patrick's parents are long gone. So are your mum and dad, God rest their souls. Who else is going to do it?'

'Right, okay,' I say, hoping that will keep her quiet for a while and she'll forget about it if I don't mention it again. And I think I've got away with it when she gets distracted by the TV and says, 'Look! A giraffe! I knew I'd seen one somewhere.'

And she's not done yet, because the next programme is an old *Top of the Pops* from the seventies, and one of the songs reminds her of the boy wonder. 'Oh, he was such a nice boy, always clean, and such nice hair, I remember.'

Hmph! *So nice he took you away from me. Remember that, do you?* I don't say it out loud, of course. I'm still hoping that if I keep my mouth shut, she'll forget it. And Patrick-Poncy-Perfect-Prick will go away.

But he never does go away. Fifty years and I still can't get rid of the annoying prat.

Meanwhile, Julie's got that puzzled look on her face again. The look that tells me that she's trying hard to remember something.

'Something's puzzling me,' she says. 'I'm trying hard to remember something. What is it now?'

I know better than to say anything to that. I don't want to encourage her.

'Do you ever wonder what things would be like if they'd turned out differently?' she asks anyway.

This time I do answer.

'How d'you mean?'

I don't like the way this conversation is going.

'Well, if Patrick hadn't died, I could have married him instead of you.'

It must be the dementia. Otherwise she'd realise that's not the kindest thing to say to a husband of forty-nine years. 'We've had a good life, haven't we?' I ask her. 'Good job, nice house, lovely children, gorgeous grandchildren, cottage in the country soon.'

'Oh, aye, but you can't help but wonder, can you?'

Can't you? I don't. I got Julie. *He* didn't. I got the wedded bliss and the *lovely home* and the *beautiful family*. *He* didn't. I'm still here. *He* isn't. I won.

Or did I? Because he's been dead fifty years but he *is still here*. Wonder Boy Patrick just *won't go away*.

But I don't say any of that either. Her dementia's been getting gradually worse. She'll forget soon. And then I'll have my peace at last.

When *Top of the Pops* finishes, she goes to one of the boxes that we haven't sealed yet, and takes out an old photo album. 'Now I remember what's puzzling me,' she says. 'These photos that your mum took of you and Patrick together. Look, there's that one of you and him playing that toy football game. Oh, and there you are covered in black muck and Patrick's standing next to that slide of his with his clean waterproofs, such a smart boy he was. I remember this one: you with your guitar and him with his organ thing. Now what was it that was bothering me?'

As annoying as it is to be reminded of my oh-so-perfect so-called pal, I don't react, still clinging to the hope that whatever was puzzling her will still be a puzzle until her dementia gets so bad that she won't even remember that there had been anything to be puzzled about.

'I've got it!' she announces. 'The's no photos of you and Patrick swimming together.'

This doesn't sound good, but it might not mean anything. She doesn't *know*. She *can't*. 'That's right. He didn't like swimming,' I say.

'But I'm sure you told me that he always did what you did, even when he didn't like it.'

Good memory for someone with dementia, but they say that their long-term memory is often okay. They just can't remember what's happened more recently. Like today. So maybe she'll forget soon. But I can tell that Julie's not going to let this one go. I'll have to put her straight.

'It was his mum,' I say. 'She reminded him that he's allergic to chlorine.'

At the time, I thought it was just an excuse because he was offended by our dirty bodies and people peeing in the pool. We used to go in dirty and come out clean. As I said, we didn't have a proper bath in the early days, we made our own entertainment.

'But he had a *boat* where he used to live, didn't he?' Julie says. 'So why didn't he swim in the river before, you know, that time, when *it* happened?'

'That's easy,' I say. 'He thought our river was too shallow and dirty compared with the one at the bottom of his garden *where he used to live*.'

Which is true, but what I'm not reminding her is that Patrick the Plank had aways worn a life jacket when he was messing about on *his* river, and he never learned to swim properly. And I'm not telling her that me and my pals had a secret spot where *our* river *was* deep enough for swimming, and that was the only thing that we managed to keep a secret from Poke-His-Nose-In-It Patrick.

'I still don't get why he went swimming with you in the river that day,' she says.

I'm trying to distract her by suggesting that we do some more packing before *Dancing on Ice* comes on; that'll keep her mind off her long-lost love. But she's not giving up.

'I mean, look at this newspaper clipping in with the photos,' she says. 'You were the hero. It says here that witnesses saw you trying to save him, pulling him out of the water and giving him mouth-to-mouth while they ran to a phone box to call the ambulance. It's what made me realise that I loved you, that it was always you. You were my hero. But why did you let him swim in the first place? Why didn't you stop him? *Why*, Johnny?'

I'm sweating now, really worried. Why does she have to look at those photos now, while she can still remember some things from ages ago? Surely she can't be onto me after all these years. What's she going to say next?

'Look, dear,' I say to her. '*Dancing on Ice* is on. Shall we watch it?'

'But we never watch the dancing together. You don't like it. Why would you do something with me that you don't like to do?'

And then her usual dazed expression becomes sharp and clear. 'Just like Patrick.'

And I've heard enough.

'Bloody Patrick! That's all I hear from you. *Patrick this, Patrick that.* After fifty years of it, it makes me sick. *You* make me sick! You're as bad as him. He was always in my face, spoiling everything, and now *you're* always in my face, going on and on about him. You'll never let me forget him, will you? You should be grateful that you ended up with me and not *him*. Have I not looked after you? Have we not had everything that we've ever wanted? *He* never cared about anyone except himself. You just can't stop harping back to Patrick Wonder Boy Perfect Prick, can you?' I stop to take a deep breath. 'So you want to know what happened, do you? Okay, I'll tell you what happened. Then maybe you'll shut up for once in your life.'

Julie cringes and presses herself back, shrinking into her favourite chair, her stupid face drained of any remaining colour.

'Here's what happened, right. When we were kids, me and my pals had a secret swimming spot in the river. It's the only thing that Patrick No Pals didn't know about. Then when he went off to uni, I used to go to this spot to swim on my own, enjoying the peace and quiet. And then when he came back from uni and went off with you, I deliberately let the secret out, knowing that he wouldn't be able to stop himself. He'd have to come and swim and try to outdo me like he always did. I knew that he was a rubbish swimmer, but I encouraged him to come anyway. A university education and he didn't suspect a thing, the plank. I had to get rid of him, you see. I couldn't let him take you away from me. And this was the easiest way to do it. I set a trap and he walked right into it. Or swam right into it, ha-ha, stupid prat. You see, there was a bend in the river where the current was stronger. You could get into trouble if you didn't know how to avoid it. And I led Patrick the Plank straight into it. You should have seen him floundering around and flapping about like a demented duck (no offence, dear). "Help me!" he was shouting. *Pathetic.* "Who? Me?" I asked him, and paddled over to the shallow part, and watched.

'When those bystanders watched me towing Pathetic Patrick to shore, he'd already drowned. When they saw me perform mouth-to-mouth I was breathing down the outside of his stupid cheek, and I wasn't putting any effort into the chest compressions either. I watched him die, and I was glad. What do you think of that?'

Julie tries to answer but there's something wrong with her mouth. One side of her face has drooped and her speech is slurring. Her old honestly-blue eyes seem to be staring in different directions. In fact, half of her body has slumped and it looks like she's losing control. There's a wet patch on her favourite chair.

I push myself out of my seat and bump into one of the stacks of boxes. By the time I've wriggled my way around the second stack, the wet patch has spread, water's dripping onto the floor, and Julie's sinking further into her chair. When I come up against the third stack, I stop.

And watch.

*

It wasn't my fault that Julie had a stroke. How was I supposed to know that she had *interrupted blood supply to the brain* as well as dementia? Poor cow. I never touched her. I only watched. *Just like I watched Patrick.* It's not my fault that she was getting all uptight about *him*. She shouldn't have been going on about Perfect (Dead) Patrick, who'd had his place in heaven for fifty years. And now Julie's there too. Good luck to them both, they deserve each other. They're probably together again now. That's if Preening

Patrick even recognises Julie after loving himself in heaven for fifty years.

Who cares? Not me, sitting quietly in my cottage in the country, all to myself.

I was never really that bothered about Julie. I only married her to get back at Patrick, even though he was already dead.

It was always about Patrick.

Everything had to be perfect for Patrick.

All I wanted was to be shot of him so that I could get some peace.

But now I've got it.

Peace, perfect peace.

After another perfect crime.

And I didn't even mean to do it this time.

I've got away with it again.

Something in the Water

Lulworth Cove, one of the most beautiful places in England, if not the world.

An almost perfect circle where millions of years ago waves battered the cliffs until a chink was created and the sea began to seep through. Their work only just started, the waves continued to pound the breach mercilessly. Rocks tumbled into the foaming water as the aperture grew wider and the advancing sea gushed between the wreckage and spread out to eventually form the cove that is so admired and loved today.

So calm, so sheltered, so at peace. Small boats barely moving, pilots surely obliged to promise that they will preserve the restfulness of the cove during their brief stay. Masts tucked away until another time, bare rigging tinkling in the slight breeze. Even the accompanying seabirds muted. Beneath these tranquil turquoise waters, darker smudges indicate miniature forests of seaweed. Reflections of sunshine and the endless blue sky that dwarfs the surrounding, towering cliffs. On one side it appears that the chalky cliffs are still sliding into the sea, and perhaps they are, although it is almost impossible to contemplate anything disturbing this perfect peace—that something so dramatic and violent from the distant past created this idyll.

There are two other main passages leading in and out of the inlet. A steep path, its broken-down steps indicating that the sea's work is not yet done, and up which energetic tourists clamber to reach a ruined schoolhouse, the world famous fossil forest and the wide and winsome Mupe Bay. But only if the red flags are not flying, because on days when the path is closed for military exercises, it is safer to remain in the cove's refuge. Finally, there is a narrow road down to the busiest part, where families gather to eat at the inevitable café, crunch their way along the pebble-strewn beach and paddle in cool, soothing waters. This secluded beach will never be a target for the usual noisy swarms of holidaymakers who invade English coasts in summer. There is no public access by vehicle, and the car park is a quarter of a mile away. People have to make an effort to reach this untroubled gem, where they can be at peace with their thoughts.

This is the scene that greets a random group of onlookers gathered at a clifftop viewpoint. It is the object of their admiration and wonder, and their contemplation. At their backs lies the Stair Hole and the Lulworth Crumple. Layers of folded strata thrust aside with disdain long ago by an almighty giant. Millions of years of pre-history, testament to a turbulent past. The Hole itself, still pounded by the sea, still crumbling. Slowly, imperceptibly, eternally, creating a new cove.

Discord behind the onlookers, harmony to their front. A collection of strangers, drawn together to this renowned sanctuary, attempting to unravel their far from peaceful thoughts. A hastily assembled cast of actors about to take to this world-famous stage. Waiting in the wings for the play to begin. Looking to the waves for answers. Beyond Lulworth Cove and the Stair Hole, staring at the open sea.

Where there is something in the water.

*

'Daddy, look! What's that out there?' asks a small boy, pointing.

'I'm not sure, Rory. What do you think it is?'

'I think it's a ship.'

'Hmm, well, it's maybe closer to shore than you think, son. Probably too small for a ship.'

'A toy ship then! Can you get it for me, Daddy? Please!'

'Well ...'

'Oh, for God's sake, Tom,' interrupts Rory's mother. 'Just tell him straight. You're not going in the water after a toy ship. Stop indulging him. And stop calling him—'

'We're only chatting, dear. It's what dads and sons do.'

'Will you *stop* calling me "dear"! I haven't been your "dear" for a long time.'

'Sorry. We're only chatting, Hattie.'

'It's Harriet!'

'Okay, okay. Sorry, *Harriet*.'

'Daddy! The ship!'

Observing this altercation from a few feet away, an elderly woman wonders what has brought the young family to this point. Are they on holiday together? Are they even together? They're clearly not getting along well. They disagree on how to speak to their son. If Rory is *their* son. He could be Tom's but not Harriet's. What has caused Harriet to react in such a way to an apparently innocuous remark about a toy ship? There must be something underneath the surface. If Harriet isn't Rory's mother, who is? Did Harriet and Tom meet after Rory was born, or did Tom have an affair, causing Harriet to carry her resentment ever since? If so, who could blame her? To the unpractised eye, Tom is the patient, indulgent father, and Harriet is the touchy, grumpy mother.

However, in the elderly woman's experience, things are never as they seem.

Her name is Hanna Heartland, an author, and she is here today to gather ideas for her next romantic mystery novel. She is wondering how to weave together this beautiful location, the relationship between Tom and Harriet and Rory, whatever is in the water, and a recent news story about a swimmer who drowned. What does Hanna think the mystery object is? She agrees with Tom that it could be a toy ship. Or is it something sinister? Could it be an item of clothing, once abandoned on the shore and now drifting out to sea? Whose clothing is it? Could it belong to the drowned swimmer? Was *Rory's real mother* that tragic victim of the sea? Spurned and abandoned by the heartless Tom, did she *take her own life*?

The new best seller by Hanna Heartland is taking shape.

A sporty-looking girl, clad in expensive Lycra cycling gear, can hardly keep her eyes off her equally expensive trail bike, chained to a sign warning of the dangers of unstable cliffs and unpredictable currents. Her partner, red-faced and winded, is dressed in a T-shirt, baggy shorts and big trainers. His rusty old commuter bike dumped on the grassy slope, he tries for the second or third time to draw the attention of the girl to whatever is in the water.

'What's that over there, Jem?'

'What? Where? Oh, that? It could be a tow float.'

'What's one of them when it's at home?'

'Keep up, Nigel. It's for open water swimming, remember? We use it for visibility and to grab onto if we get cramp. You can even keep things like car keys in it. That's what I do when I swim in the lake at home. You must remember that.'

'Now that you mention it, I think I do remember you telling me once or twice. So, what's a *tow float* doing out there?'

'Der! Somebody was swimming with it, obvs. But the question is: where's the swimmer? I'd better get down there and take a look. I fancy a swim anyway. That's why I'm wearing my tri-suit under this gear. Always prepared. You won't mind looking after my bike while I go in. It's expensive, you know.'

'But, Jem, remember that woman who drowned. Look at the *danger* notices.'

'Danger? Huh! Where's your sense of adventure, Nigel? There could be a lost swimmer out there. Somebody has to do something. You should try it sometime: doing something.'

Sitting on a rock by himself, a scruffy middle-aged man guards a frayed rucksack with a picture of a dolphin on the front. Unknown to this man, he is observed by a prim young woman, who feels in her pocket and for the fifth or sixth time this morning, pulls out an identity card and examines it with pride. Trainee Police Officer Sharon Kirrie, who has come to the cove today to practise observing people.

She has noticed the elderly woman watching Tom, Harriet and Rory with undisguised scrutiny, and she considers her own observation methods to be much more discreet. There is a story there, something behind the rift. However, she is certain that there is no perpetration of criminal activity, either by the young family or by the elderly woman, who is most probably guilty of nothing more than inquisitiveness. Just like Sharon, who is now watching Nigel trying to keep up with the overpowering Jem. They seem an unlikely couple, but not criminals, although Sharon would have to keep an eye on Jem if she really is intent on rescuing a victim at sea, imaginary or otherwise. Sharon has also heard about the woman who drowned close to this very spot. She observes the middle-aged man clutching his rucksack and watching Nigel and Jem's bikes. And she wonders why he is holding onto a dirty old rucksack like it is the most valuable thing in the world. And why he is staring at the bikes when everyone else is peering out to sea.

Her thoughts interrupted by Jem's interpretation of the mystery object, Sharon has a closer look at it. At first she thinks it is a dolphin, but that might be because she has noticed the picture on Middle-Aged Man's rucksack. Perhaps he also thinks it is a dolphin, or hopes it is. Perhaps, like Sharon, he has always wanted to see one, has always been envious of their care-free life, their freedom to go wherever the notion takes them. She has heard that dolphins are more intelligent than humans, because instead of inventing poverty, crime, wars and climate change, all they do is mess around in the waves.

However, it is only wishful thinking. It is not a dolphin. Whoever heard of an orange dolphin? Still, perhaps it is a dolphin playing with an orange tow float, and it cannot be seen because it is underwater, teasing its observers. Dolphins do that, she has read somewhere.

To return to Middle-Aged Man: he looks shifty. Sharon's people-observation skills alert her that this could be her first criminal. She is off-duty, but if this is an opportunity to discover a crime and bring the guilty party to trial, she would be a fool not to take it. Is Middle-Aged Man wishing that he was free to tease and play and have nothing to worry about? Free from what? Sharon is sure that he has committed a robbery, and now he has only two choices: get rid of what is in the rucksack (probably drugs) or keep it and get out of here fast. If he could swim well, he could stash the stuff in a tow float and escape with his imaginary dolphin friends. Or he could steal a bike. Of course it would have to be the old rusty one: he would never cut though that thick chain on the posh bike. Now, if poor, downtrodden Nigel was to unlock his oh-so-superior girlfriend's bike and—eager to please despite the way she treats him—wheel it down to the cove, no one would notice if the other bike went missing.

*

And so it is that our eight protagonists are gathered together at this spectacular viewpoint in the most idyllic of locations. All gazing at the same thing in the water. Each with a different point of view. A different part to play.

Rory, the innocent child, longing for a toy ship and a connection with his dad. Tom, the father, wanting to please his son, but aware of resentment from Harriet, his wife, clearly angry about something. Hanna Heartland, the author, lost in her fictional world, making up stories about people she does not know. Jem, the action woman, impulsive in her thrill-seeking, intolerant of the downtrodden Nigel, who is trying and failing to keep pace. Middle-Aged Man, the enigma, clinging to a bag on a rock. And Sharon Kirrie, the trainee police officer, desperate to make her first arrest.

Eight characters high above the natural amphitheatre of the cove.

Eight stories.

Eight versions of the truth.

But none of them know that there is a ninth player,

Unseen by all,

But who sees them all for who they really are.

I am that ninth protagonist.

And I see

Everything.

I see Rory, who only wants to be loved, who is not Harriet's son. Hanna Heartland was right about that. But she was wrong about Tom, who is not Rory's father. Because Rory is their long-term foster child. Tom and Harriet have been unable to have children of their own. And now Tom would like them to adopt Rory. He already calls Rory 'son' and encourages Rory to call him 'Daddy'. Which Harriet resents. Because she does not want to adopt. She wants the fostering to end. Because, after years of failed IVF treatment, she is finally pregnant. And she has not told Tom yet. Because she is scared. Scared that there will be no baby. Scared that Tom will not give up Rory. Scared of the confrontation.

And that is the story of Rory, Tom and Harriet. There is no drowned lover in this scene. But the truth is at least as tragic and mysterious as the imaginings of Hanna Heartland. Whom I also see, and wonder how the author would bring this dramatic story to a conclusion, and if the real ending will be a happy one.

I see Jem and Nigel, and I know that Jem has had something to prove since an undiagnosed condition of the joints restricted her activity in childhood. She watched in envy as her older brother went out to play, and later when he took up sport. No one understood why, in her teenage years, Jem recovered from her condition. But recover she did, and now she is making up for lost time, eager to show everyone how fit and adventurous she is. Everyone including Nigel, who is not her boyfriend, but that same older brother, now out of condition and anxiously attempting to compensate for those lost years with his sister.

According to Trainee Police Officer Sharon Kirrie, Jem and Nigel's story is of interest only because Middle-Aged Man is eying up their bikes, plotting his getaway with the stolen goods inside his rucksack.

Wrong.

Because if Sharon Kirrie's people-observation skills extended beyond Jem and Nigel, she would notice that Middle-Aged Man is also watching Rory. Gazing at him with a sadness and longing that Sharon Kirrie has missed completely. Because Middle-Aged Man is Rory's grandfather, who lost contact with his daughter, Rory's real mother, and found out only when she died that he has a grandson. Finding Rory became his passion. He tracked him down to the foster parents' home and followed them to Lulworth Cove. Where he now sits on a rock, watching them and glancing at the bikes only because they remind him that he never saw his daughter follow up her childhood interest in cycling. Hoping that he will not miss that chance with his newly discovered grandson. Inside his rucksack is a toy ship. He had no idea that Rory would point out to sea and think that he saw a ship. Is this a sign? Should he introduce himself to Tom and Harriet? He can see that they are having relationship problems, and he knows all about that. Can he help?

Middle-Aged Man's story draws this act to a close. So many stories. So many problems. So many questions.

Only one person knows all the answers.

How is it that I—seen by no one—know so much?

Who am I?

I am the ghost of the drowned swimmer.

And I see everyone and everything.

I see them all as lost souls, in turmoil, like the sea writhing in and out of the Stair Hole.

All, like the tide, at a turning point.

For Tom, Rory, Harriet and the unborn baby, the mystery object bobbing in the water is a chance to be a family at last. But if they are unable to talk about it, that chance will be swept out to sea, never to return. Middle-Aged Man's story, unlike Hanna Heartland's invention, is real. As well as the toy ship in his rucksack, he holds a lifeline to bring them all together. He could do that. Or he might unintentionally make matters worse. Perhaps he will stay away for Rory's sake. Perhaps not.

Jem sees the mystery object as a symbol of her long-lost and now rediscovered energy, whereas Nigel sees it as a risk that he will lose the sister he loved throughout her years of impairment, and still loves now after her reckless rebirth.

Sharon Kirrie, clearly with a lot to learn, has no idea what is going on.

But I do.

Because I am the ghost of *all* drowned swimmers.

I am the spirit of all lost souls.

I have lived all of their lives.

I know them all, but they cannot see me, out here, towing the float. I am invisible as I swim against the current which, after years of tormenting me, is finally, inexorably sending me towards my demise.

The final act is almost over but before the curtain falls, before my body sinks to the depths and my spirit soars to the skies, my performance today will be to save those who remain.

Up there on the clifftop, there will be a whisper in the breeze. They will all feel it, but none will know it is me. Middle-Aged Man will take the toy ship out of his bag, and the excited Rory will run towards him. Tom and Harriet will be united in their suspicion of this stranger, and then in helplessness as Rory stumbles and almost falls. Then they will be consolidated in their relief as Middle-

Aged Man instinctively grabs the child and saves him. The rescuer will stand back and watch Tom and Harriet embrace Rory and turn to thank their saviour. Both men will notice how Harriet's hands then go to her midriff. They will all look at each other with wonder, which becomes understanding. They will all talk together.

Hanna Heartland, watching the scene unfolding before her, will write her new novel, with a happy ending.

Halfway down the slope, the breeze will also reach Jem, who will stop, turn and look at Nigel with new awareness. She will see the concern and love in his eyes, and realise that her brother is not only trying to keep pace with her, but is watching over her, making sure she is safe. And at last she will feel safe in his love, will retrace her steps to the summit, and, above the soothing waters of this peaceful cove, hug her brother at last.

Trainee Police Officer Sharon Kirrie will see all of this and even understand some of it. Enough to know that here is no place to make her first arrest. Too quiet. She will stride purposefully down the steep slope to the less than quiet sound of the changing tide echoing around the Lulworth Crumple. No one will notice Sharon Kirrie's departure.

Even then no one will see me. None of them will be looking out to the open sea, where the tow float will drift out of sight, slowly, finally.

No one will see me descend—weakened, exhausted, spent—to the bottom of the sea, and ascend—recovered, redeemed, reborn—to the top of the skies.

I am the ghost of all drowned swimmers and lost souls.

My spirit will live on in those who are rediscovered, reunited, reborn.

The curtain will fall.

Until I return, to another stage and another troupe of troubled players acting out another melodrama.

I will be something in the water again.

Your Obsession

You first noticed him when you were volunteering at parkrun. But it was more than just noticed, wasn't it?

There were hundreds of parkrunners alongside him. Half of them were male. Dozens were young men of around his age. Many had that running physique that you so admire. Some had the same length or colour of hair. A few with a chiselled chin like his. He wasn't the only one.

But he was the only one you were watching.

You were supposed to encourage them all with equal enthusiasm. Newcomers especially appreciated the friendly welcome they received from volunteers and other parkrunners. They may been worried because they had never run five kilometres before. They may have felt out of place because they didn't know anyone. It was your place to reassure them and help them to feel part of the movement. A friendly gesture went a long way. That's what made them come back and keep coming back. Next time *they* could be the ones making a beginner feel at ease.

On that day, you did all of that. You easily identified the newcomers by their hesitancy, their need to find a kind face. You smiled. You showed them the course and indicated the simple, post-run checking in procedure, wished them luck. You were a good volunteer. You always were.

Then they all lined up for the start.

And you saw him.

You didn't hear anything that the run director said. Not her safety announcements, her welcome to the 'parkrun tourists' from other parkruns, her invitation to everyone to meet for a chat in the cafe after the run. Your gaze did not sweep across the mass of humanity gathered to take part in this shared activity. You didn't reflect, as you usually did, on the wide range of ages, shapes, sizes, ethnicity and social backgrounds represented on that start line. You didn't pause to wonder what made them run— for their physical, emotional or social health—or any or all of those. For every one of the hundreds of people before you, there was a unique story. But on that morning you didn't think about that. Nor did you remember to feel proud of your small part as a volunteer in making this happen. This run in the park. This simple intervention that means so much to so many.

You didn't do any of that.

Because you were staring at him.

It was easy to spot the 'regular' runners—whatever that meant now that running was more accessible and inclusive than ever before. To you, it meant the ones with a traditional distance runner's body shape. You're not supposed to say 'thin', 'slim' or 'skinny', but that's the way you saw them. And what's wrong with that? Almost in spite of their skinniness, the musculature of the regular runners' legs was well-defined while their upper bodies were relatively underdeveloped. Their lack of body fat exposed their collarbones above their running vests. You liked that.

But why him? What made him different? Was it the broad grin and pure white shining teeth? The bright blue eyes? Was it the way his hair parted neatly or that it was shaved close to his perfectly symmetrical ears? Was it his easy manner, smiling and laughing with his mates?

Your thoughts were interrupted by the run director shouting, 'Go!' And off he went. Off they all went, of course, but you were watching only him. His running style was rangy and relaxed. He seemed to float above the ground. Striding evenly, arms balanced, no unnecessary sideways movement. Efficient, beautiful running. *He* was beautiful. You wondered again why you hadn't noticed him before. Obviously he knew how to run, but maybe he was new to parkrun, or a club runner with a free weekend.

He didn't go straight to the front as you expected. With such a perfect running body and technique, it surprised you that he wasn't he up there with the leaders. Maybe he was just out for a jog, saving himself for an important race. A natural who didn't do much running, but had potential, should he want to do something about it. You'd find out later. It was your job to scan the bar codes today, you'd see his name. You could look him up online afterwards.

Meanwhile, you had to remind yourself to encourage *all* of the parkrunners as they filed past you while he settled in the top thirty or so. Still looking magnificent. Surely he was taking it easy.

After the run, as you scanned everyone's bar code on their pieces of paper, key tags or phones, you didn't look him in the eye when it was his turn. Why not? You always had a friendly, encouraging gesture for everyone. So why not for him? You smiled but couldn't manage to lift your eyes from the scanner. You tried but—as he stood in front of you smiling, breathing, perspiring—you knew that if you did look up you wouldn't be able to stop staring. You'd try and fail to deny the stirrings within you. Because of his presence. His smile. His breath. His musty smell. You couldn't talk to him, but you would look him up later.

It was the start of your obsession.

You couldn't wait to find out more about him. You knew that as soon as the results were finalised, every parkrunner would receive a text or email. If there were no anomalies, the run directors would have every single parkrunner's result available by the end of coffee. You were looking around to see if he was there, but he must have gone already. Or maybe he was in a different café. You'd have to watch him more closely next time. See where he goes.

There were no issues with the results that day and they were ready in record time. Then anyone could find out their finish position and time, and compare them with previous performances. Or with other parkrunners. Or click on any parkrunner's name to find out their age category, club (if any), performances at this parkrun and any others. Anyone could do that.

So could you.

And that's what you did, but not without first finding a quiet spot on your own to examine the results. Why didn't you do it there and then, in public? Most people at the café were on their phones, doing the same thing. Nothing wrong with that. Besides, nobody would know that you were poring over one particular parkrunner's profile. Even if they knew, it's okay, isn't it? Everybody does it. It's not like stalking. So why did you feel the need to do it privately? Were you feeling guilty, even then?

There you were, crouched in your small corner, staring at the screen. Twenty-fifth in a slow time. Or slow for someone who so looks the part. He was in the 20-24 years of age category. His 'home' parkrun was in another part of the country, where during the summer he had run only a few times. That explained it: a student, and now that term had started, he had come along to his new local parkrun. To become a regular. To join his university running team or a local club. To find a coach, and realise his obvious potential.

How to find out more. You could have asked him. But you were never going to do that, so what else could you do? Parkrun stats were transparent and accessible to all. What next?

Instagram.

Easy.

All you had to do was search for his name. Over three hundred followers. He wouldn't mind one more, would he? He probably wouldn't even notice. Even if he did, he wouldn't recognise you.

Then you looked at his posts. The usual student-type photos. Out drinking with the lads. You couldn't believe that he drank much, not with that perfect body. Then you noticed a girl in some of the photos. Blonde, curvy, long legs, false-looking boobs, pouty lips. Floozy. You're not supposed to judge, but that's how you saw her. What was she to him and he to her? Was she just one of the crowd, or something else? Who was she? Were you feeling jealous, even then?

He wasn't at parkrun on the following Saturday. You looked and looked, right up until the 9am start time, but he didn't come. Why so disappointed? You didn't even know him. Maybe so, but you couldn't wait until next week to see him again.

How else could you keep tabs on him?

Facebook.

Easy.

There he was. You read about his school; sports teams; favourite music, books and films; 'likes' and life events. There was nothing under relationship status. Even more photos and videos, further back in time. And there *she* was again, pouting, pushing her false boobs out. She didn't look his type. He looked so natural. What was he doing with the likes of *her*? Was she just a friend? One of 755 Facebook friends. So, if you invited him to be your friend, he'd probably accept. He couldn't possibly know all of those people. One more wouldn't make any difference. And of course, he wouldn't know it was you, would he?

But you didn't stop there, did you? You scrolled through his list of friends until you found *her*. With those legs, lips and boobs, she was easy to identify. She had 979 friends. So easy to make it 980. Now you could keep an eye on *her* too. See what she was up to. See what *they* were up to.

It was only a bit of online fun. You weren't actually making contact with them. Everybody does it. It's not stalking, is it?

At the next parkrun he returned wearing a university club vest. But you knew that already, because he had announced it on Instagram and Facebook. *She* wasn't running though. How could she? Those oversized boobs bouncing all over the place. *Lol.* So she wasn't there, and you had him to yourself. Well, you and a few hundred others. But by now you thought of him as yours, didn't you? You remembered that first day, when he was almost in your face, smiling, breathing, sweating. How would it have felt to touch him? If he touched you?

This time you were spared the frustration of almost close contact because you were marshalling far out on the course. You could still evaluate his running though. That's what you were doing: *evaluating,* not staring. It looked like he was running faster. He was closer to the leaders. And the results proved your theory: thirty seconds faster. How much quicker could he run? Would he enter any other competitions? You could easily find out, couldn't you?

Power of 10.

So easy.

All you had to do was enter his name and club, and there was his profile, with all his performances in competition. So far they were only parkruns, but surely he would be running cross-country with the university soon. You would have to learn patience. It was still early season. And while you were waiting, you had other information to keep you going. Photos on the parkrun website, posts on Instagram and Facebook. You'd heard of TikTok and Twitter, and were aware of other outlets for your fantasies, but you didn't know how to use them. So you made do with the photos and tried to feed your desires. You stroked the screen. But that wasn't enough for you.

Meanwhile, week by week, he was running faster and faster at parkrun, and finishing higher and higher. As you knew he would. Until one Saturday he won the race. You're not supposed to call it a race though. And you shouldn't say that he won. He was the first finisher in a timed run. It's part of the parkrun ethos. But he was the best. He must have been doing some good training at university. His teammates and maybe a coach were bringing the best out of him. It was an exciting time, but he didn't make a fuss about it. He wasn't like that.

But *she* was. It was plastered all over *her* social media accounts. About what a great runner he was. Huh! What did *she* know about it? *You* were there every week, watching and willing him on. Where was *she*? Probably at home, extracting her legs from her armpits, gluing her face on or booking another boob job. If she was even awake at that time on a Saturday morning. Hmph! She was getting ideas above her station. You would have to watch her more closely.

Meanwhile, you checked Power of 10 at least twice per week. His cross-country performances started to appear. He made a promising debut, then improved in his second race. Months passed. He ran some road races too, and a track race indoors.

By that time he wasn't running a parkrun every week. Which spoiled your Saturday mornings. Parkrun had been the only reason you got out of bed on a Saturday; then it was to see him, even though you still didn't talk to him. So you checked the university fixture list and followed him to his races. He didn't know you were there, of course. You kept yourself hidden while he battled through the rain, hail, wind and snow. So did you, to get there. Not *her*, though. Rain, hail, wind and snow—*her*? Too precious about her looks. *You* gave up your day for him. You planned your journeys to the venues, found good places to hide. But you were still exposed to the elements, weren't you? What if you exposed yourself to more than the elements? What if, naked, you jumped out in front of him and shouted, *Look at me! I'm yours! Come and get me!* But you wouldn't do that to him. You cared too much to put him off his race. Or to put him off you.

Even so, you knew that he wouldn't run well if you weren't there to support him. He needed you, and you needed him. After all those months, it was obvious that you needed each other. You knew that. He did too. Or he would do if he knew who you were. But you were never going to make that happen. You wouldn't contact him on social media, couldn't say hello, wouldn't introduce yourself. So you carried on following him.

But it wasn't stalking, was it?

Everyone does it.

There's no *law* against it, is there?

You were only following him on social media and then supporting him at races.

And you kept your thoughts to yourself.

Everyone has fantasies.

What's wrong with that?

And then you started to follow him around campus. You weren't going to *do* anything, of course. You only wanted to see more of him. You'd have liked to see more of him, wouldn't you? But you weren't going to peer through windows. You wouldn't do anything to cause him distress. You loved him too much. Yes, you loved him. And he loved you. He just didn't know it yet. Because he didn't know you.

You kept on following. And watching. You watched, camera at the ready as he left the halls of residence. You followed him as he walked to lectures. You were already there when he went to the refectory for lunch. You watched him eat, and you wished you were inside that mouth. You followed him back to the halls and you watched him at athletics training. He was poetry on the track. He was sexual as he recovered, legs quivering, chest rising and falling, panting. You wished that *you* made him feel like that.

You went home with your new photos, stroked the screen again and touched yourself. You fantasised about touching him and about how he would respond. Would he touch you? What part of you would he touch first?

He never noticed you.

Not even when you followed him home in the dark.

Until something changed.

It was *her* fault.

She made you do it.

You didn't mind when he chatted with his friends at lunchtime, or when he trained with others on the track. You didn't mind when he walked home in a group from training. You didn't even mind when he socialised in the student bar with friends.

Until one night, when *she* walked home with him. Tipsy, wobbling precariously on high heels, legs even longer than usual, no surprise in a skirt that short. Glossy, sparkling legs, almost all the way up to her glossy, sparkling, pumped-up boobs, just under her glossy, sparkling, pumped-up lips. False eyelashes fluttering underneath tumbling, platinum-blonde hair. It wasn't exactly a student look. All the other female students were in jeans and hoodies. What was *she* even doing there? *She* wasn't a student.

She must have been visiting him.

You wondered again, didn't you: what was she to him and he to her?

And you followed them both home, together.

Of course you did.

She was leaning against him. He put his arm around her. It could have been to stop her falling over. He could have been just helping a friend. But she was gazing up at him, staring into his eyes. She didn't have a right to stare at him, but *you* did, didn't you? At the door he fiddled with his keys with one hand while holding her steady with the other. She was clinging, staggering, swaying, boobs wobbling like jelly. Still staring at him. The only thing about her that was still was her stare.

It should have been you. You should have been clinging to him. *You* should have been gazing into his eyes. If it was you, he wouldn't have been fumbling with his keys, not looking at the person under his arm. He would turn and *fumble* with you, kiss you, whisper in your ear, open the door in no time, lead you upstairs.

To his room. Your fantasy would come true. He would be yours and you would be his. As you always were. As you were meant to be. Forever.

But it was *her*. Not you. He walked through the doorway and *she* stumbled through it. You couldn't see what happened next, but you imagined them making their way together upstairs, one teetering, the other supporting. You imagined them hesitating outside his door as he felt his way into the keyhole.

Stop!

You had to stop imagining. You were gasping for breath, heart thumping, face flushed, panicking. A palpitating wreck. You had to hold onto a lamp post to steady yourself. You needed to make your way home before someone spotted you. Seeing you in that state, a well-meaning bystander might even have called an ambulance. You couldn't let that happen. Your cover would be blown. You wouldn't be able to keep doing *this*. You had to get home, recover, and plan your next move.

You would have to do something about *her*.

*

Weeks passed, and you still hadn't made contact with him.

But that was about to change.

Warnings. All over social media. *Be careful when you go out at night on campus*. Even *he* posted something. First of all, when his kit bag went missing at the track. Someone had seen a stranger loitering nearby.

It was you, wasn't it? You wanted to feel closer to him, but you couldn't talk to him, so you took his bag home with you instead. There was no harm in that, was there? To him, they were only some old clothes. To you, they were nectar. You breathed in his smell, rubbed his clothes against you, licked them, wore them.

More warnings. Some weirdo hanging around campus, taking photos. That was you too, wasn't it? You'd been noticed, outside the lecture theatres with your notebook; in the refectory with your flat white; passing by the halls of residence, trying to look like you were going somewhere; clutching your phone while sheltering under your umbrella at the track. But you always got away before anyone challenged you. And he didn't know it was you, so it was okay, wasn't it?

Until *she* came back to visit again. What did *she* ever do for him? Why did she have to keep turning up, all flirty and starry-eyed? *You* were the one who was always there for him. On campus day and night, at the track in all weathers, in faraway muddy fields. *You* were dedicated. *She* wasn't. She thought she could just rock up in her ridiculous high heels, short skirt and big eyelashes and grab all the attention. You had to teach her a lesson. She had to understand that he was yours and you were his. She was nothing. She needed to stay out of your way.

Even more warnings. Desperate. *Be on your guard, especially at night. Don't go out alone. There's a weirdo on the loose.*

And he posted: *My friend was accosted by a stalker. If you saw what happened or if you see anything suspicious in the future, tell the police. This person is dangerous and has to be stopped.*

Stalker? You're not a stalker, are you? You were just taking an interest in the wellbeing of someone special. *You* knew what was best for him. You knew *who's* best for him. That's not stalking, is it?

Accosted? All you did was approach her. She had to know what—*who*—was best for him, and that it wasn't her: it was you. She read the signals straightaway. She gasped, backed away, and then went crying to *him*. Mascara running down her pumped-up face, lips-a-quiver, like her boobs. *Oh, poor me! I was threatened by the big bad stalker!*

Threatened? You didn't *threaten*, did you? You just *approached* her. And you hardly touched her. The wimp.

Dangerous? Who? *You*?

But you must have scared her off, because she went home again.

*

And now it's just you and him.

Finally you'll have him alone.

So here you are, ready to go out at night again.

It's time.

First of all you have to say goodbye to your mum. Tell her you're just popping out for a while, you won't be long. And your mum says what she always says: *Be careful. Remember what happened that night.*

That night. It was over *forty years ago*, and she says the same thing every time you go out at night. What does she know? She's eighty-five. *Remember what happened.* She can't recall what happened yesterday. But she remembers what happened to you that night over forty years ago.

Forty years ago.

You'll never forget, will you?

Endless nights of being watched, followed, stalked.

Until *that* night, when *your* stalker stopped being only a stalker.

And became something infinitely worse.

You remember what happened, of course you do.

How it affected you, how it affects you still.

How you haven't uttered a word *for forty years.*

You've never had a partner.

Nobody wants you.

You should have been a parent long ago.

Your children would have been about *his* age by now.

But you still live with your mum.

You don't do anything.

You can't even speak.

You just watch.

And follow.

Until now.

Now that you've got *Blonde Bimbo* out of the way.

Now that you're in control.

That's why you're going out in the dark again tonight.

Back to the university.

Where *he'll* be on his own, beautiful, *yours.*

What are you going to do?

You won't do anything to harm him, will you?

Because you know how *that* feels, don't you?

But you'll finally show him how you feel about him.

How you've always been there for him.

Watching over him, caring for him, *loving* him.

It's always been you and it's always been him.

How will he react, and how will you respond?

Will you still be *in control* then?

Of course not.

You'll stop pretending that you're doing it all for him.

You'll think only of yourself.

You'll do something you'll regret forever.

You won't believe that the police will catch you.

Because they didn't catch *your* stalker forty years ago, did they?

But they'll catch *you.*

And you'll be handcuffed and shivering in an empty room.

Staring at the blank walls.

While, next door, the police will be putting the pieces together.

They'll blame you for what happened.

But they won't know *why* you did it, will they?

Only you'll know that,

but it won't matter anymore,

because
after forty years,
at last
you'll know:
it's over.

A Disappearing Elephant

'Are you sure that was a good idea, Guv?' asked the police sergeant, slicking back his greased hair.

'Eh? Well, you know what these educated university-types are like,' answered the dishevelled inspector, brushing ash from the sleeves of his crumpled jacket. 'Think they know it all. Think they're getting down with the plebs, working their way up through the ranks.'

'It's only his first week, though, Guv. Seems a bit rough on the lad.'

'If he wants to learn on the job, he'll have to take the rough with the smooth, won't he?'

'How long do you think it will take him to realise, Guv?'

'What? That we're pulling his leg?'

'Yes, Guv. Anyone with one iota of common sense knows a cock and bull story when they hear one, but you know what these new guys are like: they'll do anything to please.'

'That's the trouble, Sergeant: just because he's got a university degree doesn't mean that he's got any sense. Unless disappearing elephants are common occurrences at Oxbridge, that is. I mean, they're all on drugs, these students, aren't they?'

*

Sounds like a wild elephant chase to me, thought the young constable as he cycled to the park. *Residents see an elephant trampling down their gardens but when they look again, the elephant has mysteriously disappeared. How can an elephant disappear in the middle of a city? How did it get there, anyway? If there even is one, which I seriously doubt. I should visit the residents who made the reports, and then maybe ask at the zoo. Not meet a gardener at the city park, but that's where the guv's sent me. And it's my first case, my chance to show what I'm made of. I know what they say about me: they think that because I'm educated, I'm not practical. They think that a practical man like the city gardener will know what to do, and all I'm good for is taking notes and reporting back. Well, we'll see about that.*

*

The city park gardener looked up from his flowerbeds to see a young, athletic-looking constable wearing a brand new uniform and parking his bike outside the pavilion next to the allotments. *Looks like one of these clever clogs,* he thought.

'Good morning, sir,' said the constable cheerfully. 'Fine day! I understand that you're the gardening expert around these acres.'

Expert, eh? Trying to butter me up, is he? thought the gardener. *These acres? I suppose he thinks that's gardening-speak. Hmph!* 'Good morning, Constable,' he replied politely. 'What can I do for you?'

'Well, it sounds pretty unlikely, if you ask me,' said the constable.

I didn't ask you, thought the gardener.

'But you must have heard the stories of a disappearing elephant,' the constable continued.

'I've heard.'

'What do you reckon?'

'A load of old codswallop,' answered the gardener.

'My thoughts entirely.'

Hmph! Thinks he can win me over by agreeing with me, thought the gardener, unswayed.

'But if there were any truth in the stories,' continued the constable, 'why would all the sightings be in gardens? What would you suggest?'

'Have you tried the zoo? Any escaped elephants with an interest in gardening?'

'Ha-ha, not likely. But you're right, it makes perfect sense to visit the zoo. Thank you for your help.'

Hasn't a clue, thought the gardener as he watched the constable cycle off. *Is that the best the constabulary can give us nowadays? God help us all!*

*

Hmm, thought the constable as he cycled across the city towards the zoo. *How odd that he didn't suggest asking the people who own the gardens, before he sent me to the zoo. It seems that I'm pursuing my line of enquiry in the wrong order. Never mind, the zoo's on my way to the trampled gardens. Hmm, that's odd too: the gardens aren't close to the zoo. So, even if an elephant did escape, why didn't it wreck the gardens nearest to the zoo? Oh well, maybe the zoo keeper can throw some light on the mystery. Something tells me that there's more to this than meets the eye.*

By lunchtime, the constable was none the wiser. Of course there were no escaped elephants from the zoo. And no, the zoo keeper had no idea why people would report sightings of an elephant in their gardens. It sounded like a cock and bull elephant story to him.

Very droll, thought the constable. *Everyone's a comedian today. Nothing to it but to visit the residents now, which is what I should have done in the first place. Maybe they'll offer sandwiches to their friendly bobby on the beat. I'm starving. All this biking is giving me a good appetite. But what a life! Out in the fresh air, enjoying the summer, searching for a wayward elephant. What better way to begin my career in the police force?*

*

‘Ooh yeah, I seed an elephant all right,’ said the first resident, smoothing down her apron and patting the rollers in her hair as the constable gratefully gobbled down tea and sandwiches from the only person to give him a warm welcome so far. ‘Last night it was. Right in front of me eyes, as sure as I sees you sittin’ on me couch now. Except I was lookin’ out of me window, of course. Dark it was, but I knows an elephant when I sees one: I’ve watched Richard Attenborough on TV. There it was, large as life, tramplin’ me plants down like billio and kickin’ up dirt every which way. And then I went to get me phone, and the bloomin’ elephant had disappeared! But I’ll tell you now, I weren’t mistaken. How else would you explain the mess in my garden?’

The constable had to agree that the garden was a bit of a mess. Plants ripped up, earth overturned and soil scattered. Oddly though, no trampled down fences, and no actual elephant mess. No *great* damage, in fact, so why an elephant? Nevertheless it was the same story from all of the affected residents, although it was strange that, of the neighbours whose gardens were *un*disturbed, not one had seen or heard anything. What was going on? But there was nothing more to be done today. It was nearing the end of the afternoon and he had to make his report.

*

'So, the new guy's started quite well, Guv,' said the sergeant, sipping his seventh cup of coffee of the day.

'Not too bad,' concurred the inspector, slurping his and spilling it over his already grubby sleeve. 'New guys, eh? Yeah, this one's doing okay, considering it was supposed to be a joke.'

'You think he might be on to something, Guv?'

'You never know, Sergeant. He's methodical, I'll give him that. Maybe we'll find out more after he interviews the residents again tomorrow. Maybe he's got more sense than we gave him credit for.'

*

'Sorry to disturb you again so soon, madam,' said the constable, from the doorstep. 'Do you mind if I ask you a few more questions about the disturbance in your garden?'

'No trouble at all, Constable. I'll put me kettle on. Would you like mint tea this time? I picked some mint this mornin' from me garden. What's left of me garden, that is. Bloomin' elephant!'

'Oh, no thanks. Just ordinary tea for me, please.'

'To be honest, I prefers ordinary tea in the mornin' meself. I likes me mint tea in the evening, I does.'

Half an hour later, while watching the constable knocking on a neighbour's door, she thought to herself, *What a nice, handsome young fella. He can come round any time. Nice of him to take an interest in me garden. I never dreamed that our local bobby would want to know so much about herbs.*

*

'And they all said the same thing, did they?' asked the inspector later.

'Much the same, sir,' answered the constable.

'And you think the gardener will confirm your suspicions?'

'It would seem to make sense, sir.'

'It's worth a try, Guv,' added the sergeant. 'Why don't I accompany the constable? If he's really on to something, he might need backup.'

*

The guv doesn't have time for graduates, thought the sergeant as he parked the squad car at the pavilion. *But he might regret playing a joke on this new guy. If his theory's correct, the joke'll be on the guv.*

'Okay, Constable,' said the sergeant, spotting the gardener with sleeves rolled up and cap pushed back on his head, busy with his flower beds, 'you do the talking. I'll be right here if you need me.'

'Thanks, Sarge. I won't let you down. Hello again, sir!' he called to the gardener. 'Another fine day!'

'Back so soon, Constable?'

'Indeed. Just wanted to ask you a few more questions if I may.'

Confident, thought the sergeant. *Good start. The gardener's looking shifty, though.*

'As lovely as your flower beds are, I'd be grateful if you showed us your herb garden, please.'

'Eh?'

'I've heard that it is quite expansive. Must be a good business you have going here.'

Nice line, thought the sergeant. *That's raised the gardener's hackles. He's not happy, but he can hardly deny such a reasonable request.*

'It's *huge,*' exclaimed the constable, looking over row upon row of neatly arranged green plants. 'I've never seen so much … mint. It *is* mint, isn't it? They must love their mint tea here.'

'Erm, I suppose they do.'

'And those mounds of earth on the other side of the fence. You supply fine quality soil to the locals, I believe?'

'Nowt but the best.'

'The best. Indeed. And do you also supply mint?'

'Not if I can help it. Much better if they grow their own.'

'Grow their own. Indeed. I wonder why you need so much of it here. Hmm …'

Keep it going, lad, thought the sergeant. *You're reeling him in. That gardener's looking really nervous now. Seems to be staring at something behind us.* The sergeant couldn't help turning around. *Nothing there.*

'On the other hand,' the constable went on, 'mint tea is a local speciality, wouldn't you agree?'

'Erm …'

'You see,' explained the constable, 'I've been chatting to the residents whose gardens were disturbed, and it's a funny thing …'

In for the kill, lad.

'They all have herb gardens, they all drink mint tea, and they all get their soil from you.'

'I never supplied no mint!' the gardener insisted.

'But you did supply soil.'

What is *that gardener staring at?* wondered the sergeant again. *Got to hand it to the lad, though. Hasn't looked back once. Really focused.*

'And seeing how close your piles of soil are to your … mint. Can you see what I'm getting at, sir?'

'Eh?'

'I suggest to you, sir, that seeds from your *mint* have made their way into your soil, and therefore into the residents' herb gardens.'

'Can't be helped. Nowt wrong with that.'

'Except that it isn't mint, is it, sir? It's something that looks a bit like mint, isn't it?'

Brilliant performance, thought the sergeant. *I've never seen a suspect look so guilty: sweating, twitching, staring behind us. His eyes are nearly popping out of his head!*

'*Hierba de la Pastora* (*Salvia divinorum*),' said the constable. 'But you knew that already, didn't you, sir?'

'It was an accident!' protested the gardener. 'They wasn't supposed to get their plants mixed up! How was I to know they'd put it in their tea?'

'But you knew it could cause hallucinations, didn't you, sir? So, why grow it at all?'

'I couldn't help it! It's *his* fault!' the gardener yelled, quivering, staring open-mouthed and pointing at something high in the air behind the two police officers. 'It was the elephant! He made me do it! He threatened me! Told me that if I didn't supply his herd, they'd trample me to death!'

'That, sir, is what comes of taking drugs: one thing leads to another. I'm arresting you on suspicion of supplying illegal drugs …'

*

'It was impressive, Guv,' stated the sergeant, back at the station. 'The constable just ground him into submission.'

'Thanks, Sarge,' said the constable, blushing.

'I may have underestimated you, Constable,' admitted the inspector. *I'm going to have to eat humble pie here,* he thought.

'Thank you, sir.'

'Who'd have thought that there was a major drug deal going on under our noses in *this* city?' said the inspector. 'Nothing ever happens here, but you found out that mint was growing in all of the disturbed gardens, and that all the owners drank mint tea. And this other herb got mixed up with their mint, and that caused the hallucinations. And they all got their soil from the same gardener, who didn't supply the plants on purpose. But you suspected that, with so much of the stuff, he must have been supplying drugs to *someone*.'

'Yes, sir.'

'And when the gardener realised his mistake, he sneaked into the gardens at night, and tried to dig up the evidence.'

'Yes, sir.'

'And the elephant made him do it.'

'Apparently so, sir.'

'Sorry, Constable, I have to ask you this: how did you know about this hallucinatory plant? Did you take drugs when you were a student? Don't worry, it won't be held against you.'

'Oh no, sir. I studied Botany.'

Good God, thought the inspector. *I'm being upstaged by a young whippersnapper who spent his student days sniffing flowers.* 'You can stop sniggering now, Sergeant,' he said and, turning back to the constable, asked, 'One more question: why elephants? Why did they all have the same hallucination?'

'Dynasties, sir.'

'I told you to stop sniggering, Sergeant! Dynasties, Constable?'

'Yes, sir. It's the new David Attenborough series on TV. On the night in question, they all watched the episode about elephants.'

'We should watch it, Guv,' suggested the sergeant. 'It's educational. We could all le—'

'That's enough, Sergeant!' interrupted the inspector, thinking: *Education and common sense, eh? They do go together, after all. That'll teach me to make assumptions. This new constable is going to keep me on my toes. I'll have to get myself educated to keep up. Maybe a part-time course or something.*

Now, how do I find David Attenborough on BBC iPlayer?

Nae Respect

It was 1975. Things were different then. Or were they? People were much the same. How people treated other people wasn't so different from today. And how people felt about how they were treated was also the same.

Sometimes feelings last a lifetime. You look back and wonder why they remain to this day. What was so traumatic that you acted in the way that you did, and can't forget what you did? Was it worth it?

Here's what happened. Judge for yourself.

*

Y'know when you leave school and go to work in an office, you don't expect people to behave like undisciplined kids, do you? You expect them to be civilised, y'know, with respect for others and that. I mean the better you work the more money you earn, what with promotion and that. Well it's not like school, is it? Where it was the in thing to play up to teachers. I suppose we thought we were so clever back then. Well some of us did. Others just mucked about because everybody else did it and they didn't want to be called swots or sooks. The problem then was that we just weren't mature enough to realise that when we tried to make a fool of a teacher and that, we were only making fools of ourselves, because not many people can pass exams by messing around all the time, can they? Besides it's just not nice doing something like that to a teacher who's only trying to help us. I mean we must have really hurt some of our teachers by being rude to them and all that but we didn't even think about how they felt getting up in the morning after disturbed sleep to face us every day. It must have been a nightmare for them. *We* were a nightmare. We didn't show respect for a fellow human being. It was a shame really and I wouldn't do anything like that again. If I was teaching a bunch of kids who not only wouldn't work or help themselves but who actually made it impossible for anyone else to get on, I'd get mad. I'd really hate those kids.

What I'm really trying to say is that not everybody learns when they get older. Some stay exactly the same and some get worse. Like when you phone up an office and the person on the other end of the phone is oh so polite—'Yes sir, certainly sir, I hope that will be all right for you, sir, a pleasure to help you, sir'—and all that crap, do you ever stop to think what that person is really like? Do they really mean what they say? Would they do the same for you if you lived in a different part of the city or whatever? I suppose you're wondering what I'm on about. Well there's me and some other folk working in an office …

I suppose the arguments started only a few days after I began working in this insurance office in the big shitty. And now there's this big row brewing up that's going to be a whole lot worse than all the other rows put together. Or maybe not that much worse but it seems that all the others have been leading up to this one. It's like a volcano shuddering, knocking people about and then finally blowing up and causing havoc and wrecking stuff all over the place.

This day I'm telling you about starts like every other day. Get up, have breakfast, get dressed and all that stuff, walk to the train station and get on the 8.15am train, just like a clockwork toy. Now, our town's station is quite nice really. It's got flowers and friendly attendants who always say, 'Good morning, sir, how are you today?' like they really mean it. It sort of cheers you up in the morning when you're not really looking forward to another day in that hellhole of an office.

The train takes about twenty-five minutes to reach the city centre and I swear that the scenery gets more depressing the closer to the office it gets. Before you get to the outskirts it's not too bad. I mean there's a couple of nice parks and some fields and trees but then your mood plummets when you're surrounded by high-rise flats and factories and chimneys belching smoke all over the place and scrapheaps and smashed-up houses and wasteland and all that. It depresses the hell out of you, it really does. And another thing that gets worse as you get nearer to the city centre is that there's never enough room on the train for new people to get on. Our station's at the other end of the line so we're okay but after about three stops the folk getting on can't sit together, then a couple of stops later there's no seats at all and after that there's hardly room to stand and everyone's crammed together breathing each other's breath and smelling each other's smells. If cows or sheep were packed in like that, the RSPCA and all them would kick up stink. And then some clown lights up a fag—in a non-smoker compartment, which really gets on my wick—and he blows it all over your face and hair and tips ash on your trousers and that and you come off the train coughing and smelling like you've walked through a bonfire or something. It really annoys you, so it does.

Anyhow, this particular morning, quite early in the journey before it gets really busy, it's my bad luck to be sitting opposite one of these old guys who just can't mind his own business. This one takes it upon himself to tell the ticket inspector what he thinks about some younger passengers. 'You're the ticket inspector,' he says. 'Do you not think it's ridiculous the way those young people have got their luggage all over the seats? That lady had to move a bag out the way before she could sit down. It's ridiculous!' The ticket inspector mumbles something about *not his job* and then shuffles up the passageway and asks the young people to put their luggage up on the rack, which they do straightaway.

'That was really annoying me,' the busybody says to the guy sitting next to him. 'Those young people made no effort to help that lady. They just sat there laughing.'

Now I'm thinking that this is all a big fuss about nothing because this early in the journey there's plenty of room for the lady to sit somewhere else and in any case the young people moved their luggage as soon as they were asked, so they would have done the same if the lady had asked them. And I'm sure they weren't laughing at her anyway, they were just laughing with each other. Okay they could have put their bags up in the first place and they didn't but that's not too bad, is it? But Mr Busybody had to stick his nose in where it wasn't wanted because he was annoyed but he wouldn't have thought of asking the young people politely, would he? Oh no, he had to clipe on them to the ticket inspector.

Anyway the old guy next to him agrees and says, 'It's typical though, is it no'? Nae respect fur onybody nowadays.'

Obviously, he's talking about the young generation but how typical of *his* generation that he lumps us all together. I mean I'm a member of the young generation and he must know I can hear him but he's not showing any respect for me, is he? But I'm not saying anything because I don't want to get into a row. Besides, I don't want to lump all *old* people together because that would make me the same as them, wouldn't it? And they do have a point: there are people who have 'nae respect for onybody nowadays', plenty of them. There's those schoolkids I was telling you about but it's not only young people, because some folk never learn. Like there's those know-it-alls who think they can do anyone's job better—always criticising doctors, teachers, social workers—people who do difficult jobs and try their best, most of them. Or slagging off students, Asians, Catholics, Protestants; you name them, they slag them. And worse, what do some folk do when the police and the army try to protect us? Throw bricks and bottles at them. It depresses me, it really does, I can tell you.

The train eventually pulls into the city centre station and what an eyesore it is. You've endured a journey of smoke, smells, moaning and groaning, all kinds of stuffiness, dismal views out of the window and what greets you when you get off? Rubbish scattered all over the platform, piled up dirt, mucky puddles. Draughty, dingy, dank and downright depressing. This day isn't getting any better and it's only 8.45am.

It's a relief to get past the ticket collector—who must be fed up with leaning on his elbow in exactly the same position every day—and out into the square where you can see the pigeons. I like pigeons. I wish I could take off and fly with them up and away over the buildings and out into the countryside and not bother with the office for at least one day. But these city pigeons have a rough time because people complain that they make a mess (which is a laugh when you see the mess that people make) so they put wire nets up to stop them landing on buildings and they get caught in the wire and fly off minus a toe or worse. It's shame for the poor wee souls. At least some people still feed pigeons, which is being considerate, I suppose, even if they don't know what's good for them.

I'm in the office reception and saying good morning and some folk are saying good morning back. Some of them are okay, although they all talk about you behind your back of course, and nearly everyone only says good morning through habit. When they ask how you are or if you've had a nice weekend you can tell they couldn't care less how you are or if you've had a nice weekend. I try not to ask how someone is or if they've had a nice weekend unless I really want to know but it's easy to slip into the habit like everyone else does.

Anyway here I am faced with a pile of untouched mail. Let me explain how things work in this place. I'm one of the clerks who does the paperwork for the inspectors, who are really salesmen because they go out and sell insurance policies and that, but inspector sounds better, I suppose. Each inspector deals with a certain part of the city. There's three of us in our team of clerks—Dave, Joyce and me—each of us working with a different inspector. Today, after half an hour or so, the manager, Richard, comes round to tell me that Dave has phoned in sick. Now Richard can either give Dave's work to me and Joyce or to the other team, which hasn't had much work for a while. The logical thing to do is to give the work to the least busy team and that's what Richard is about to do. Until I make a stupid mistake. I don't wait for Joyce (who works part-time) to come in. I say, 'It's okay, it looks like Joyce and I won't be too busy today, so we'll manage Dave's work too.'

You should see the relief on Richard's face, and here's why he feels that way: if he gives Dave's work to the least busy team it means that Russ and Gail will be doing it and they, to say the least, are awkward. Russ is a couple of years older than me and has greasy hair and skin, unpressed clothes, hands permanently in his pockets, slouches all the time and never lifts a finger to help anyone. He's content to spin his work out and even hides client cards in his drawer so that he can get overtime to file them later. And what's worse is he likes to provoke me from time to time because I'm the youngest. I try not to let it bother me too much, pretend to laugh it off as banter. As long as you don't ask him to do any work that doesn't belong to his inspector he mostly ignores you and doesn't give you any trouble. That's how he is most of the time anyway but sometimes he erupts into a violent temper and it takes a brave man or an idiot to approach him. I don't really like him that much because he's a pretty horrible bloke, y'know?

Gail isn't that nice either but in a different way. She's nice-looking and that and she's a good worker but she knows it and never admits a mistake. If you suggest that she's made even a teeny weeny error, she denies it and accuses you of anything she can think up to make her seem in the right. Then she loses the rag at the slightest thing. Once I had to ask her if she knew anything about a particular client case and she got it into her head that I was accusing her of something so she started shouting and throwing personal insults at me. I wasn't accusing her of anything, I just wanted to know something. I'd tell you more but you might feel sick and you've got enough on your plate with this story as it is.

All in all, these two people weren't very nice, y'know what I mean?

When Joyce arrives she's not happy with me for taking on the extra work. She reminds me that although there's not much in the mail there will probably be a lot of phone calls and our inspectors will probably bring work in later. There's also our local brokers who are always coming into the office two or three times a day expecting work to be done there and then. Of course I know all this already and Joyce is nice about it and that—she's a nice person and we get on well—but I'm starting to feel guilty and worried. The only reason that I've offered to take on Dave's work is that I didn't want to start a row. I knew that Russ and Gail would have kicked up stink if they had to do someone else's work. I only wanted to work in peace but I should have kept my mouth shut like I did on the train. It could have saved a whole lot of trouble. Which is starting to bubble up.

Of course Joyce is right. There is a lot of phone calls, our inspectors do bring more work, and those brokers do drop in with their urgent demands. Dave's inspector is busy too. Before long we have too much work to do. And most of the things that annoy me about the office are happening around me. Inspectors and brokers pushing you to get it done right now and then getting stroppy when you're not quick enough and you miss their deadlines. To be honest with you, I don't think that their clients are in that much of a hurry to get the information from us; it's just the inspectors and brokers trying to impress them so that they can earn their commission, even if it means treating us like dirt.

And then there's the clerks who spend about half an hour standing at the photocopier, backstabbing someone who isn't there, like a typist or the manager or even the new Miss World—anyone. Like I said, you name them, they slag them. And half the time these gossips are all too scared to go back to work in case the rest of them slag them off when they've gone. And then in the middle of all that gossiping you'll get the receptionist phoning through to say that there's some guy on the line asking for information and one of the gossips will say, 'What does he want? Where does he live? Whereabouts? That's not my area. Not my work.' Blah blah blah. Then they'll put the phone down and say, 'Huh! It wasn't even my work!' And they'll spend the next ten minutes slagging off the receptionist. You might say I'm exaggerating but I've seen this happen time and time again. It's amazing that any work gets done at all, so it is.

Anyway, Joyce and I are having a hectic time of it with all the work coming in, and the backstabbing is really getting me down. It feels like someone's pressing heavy weights onto my head from all sides. And I've got a feeling that it's only going to get worse. Then our favourite brokers tell us to get a quote ready by 4.30pm and it's 3.55pm and it'll take half an hour to get the thing done and Joyce finishes at 4pm so I have to drop everything and get this quote prepared. And then, wouldn't you know it, Dave's inspector appears demanding a quote by 4.45pm so that's another case of dropping everything and all that. Which I can't do because I've already dropped everything for that other thing, y'know? So who's going to do the new thing? Guess who? Yep, and that's where the *real* trouble begins. Somebody has to ask Russ or Gail. So Richard takes a deep breath and, quivering (poor bloke), he asks Russ, 'Would you do this quote? Everyone else is too busy.'

Then that volcano I was telling you about has its first rumble. If it was any other volcano that would have been the end of it. Erupted, done and dusted, settled down. But Russ is no ordinary volcano. He's only warming up. 'WHAT?' and the inevitable, 'It's not my work.' And then, 'That idiot in the corner (that's me he's taking about) said he was going to do Dave's work today.'

'Well, he *has* been doing it but he's got too much on now and Joyce is going home, so can you do it?' said Richard, tossing the quote request onto Russ's desk.

And then Gail has to butt in: 'The idiot in the corner said he'd do it, so why not let him do it? He can't change his mind now.'

That's twice I've been called an idiot and I'm getting upset to be honest. And the principle of the thing is getting to me. 'For goodness sake,' I said, 'you're only being asked to do one quote. Joyce and I have been doing Dave's work all day. Can you not do this one thing?'

Which was my second big mistake of the day.

'The point is,' began Gail, and you just know it's not going to be the point at all, 'you said this morning you'd do it and you can't go changing your mind and putting on us now.'

'Look!' shouted Richard. 'Just do it! Russ or Gail, get it done, will you?'

'I'm doing my own work first,' claims Russ.

But Richard isn't going to stand for this, which is pretty unusual for him because he's a quiet bloke and usually too soft. 'You'll do that quote first! It's urgent! When I say I want it done now, it means *do it now*!' Which is funny in a way because he hadn't actually said that he wanted it done now. I say it's funny but it really isn't. This whole thing is one of the most unfunny things ever to happen to me. It's horrible and it's making me feel sick. Sick of the row, sick of the office, sick of the job, sick of the city, sick of everything.

Russ on the other hand thinks it's *really* funny. 'Don't hit me, Richard, don't hit me!' He pretends to cower and then smirks and, as slowly as possible, picks up the request slip.

At this point Joyce, who has been very quiet, has to go, saying how sorry she is to leave me at a time like this but she has a dental appointment and can't be late and hopes things work out okay for me. 'Just do as much as you can,' she advises. 'We'll get on with the rest of the work tomorrow. Dave will probably be back in the morning, so we'll be okay.'

It's like one of those Shakespeare plays when someone says, 'All may yet be well.' And you know fine that all's not going to be well at all. Boy, am I miserable. My face feels like it's boiling and my mind's full of all the unfair things I've heard today and I can't think straight. I'm walking over to a filing cabinet to look something up and because I'm distracted and not walking at the speed of light, Russ turns to Gail and says sarcastically, 'He looks busy, doesn't he?'

I try to ignore him and get on with the work and I try to do the same when Gail says, 'The thing is, you just can't change your mind later in the day, can you?'

And then Russ replies, 'What do you expect from the idiot in the corner?'

And I blow up.

'If you've got something to say, say it to me! I'll give you something to talk about!'

'*You?*' Russ laughs.

And there's nothing worse than having a threat laughed at but before either of us can say anything else, Richard bursts onto the scene. 'BLOODY WELL SHUT UP AND GET THAT QUOTE DONE, RUSS!'

If Richard was the sort who yelled like that now and again and this was a normal office, everyone would have been subdued into getting their heads down and on with their work but as you've probably gathered by now this is no ordinary office, so Russ stays slouched in his chair, smirking, a bloodshot eye winking at Richard, clicking his pen in and out, acting dead nonch until he probably thinks that he's asserted himself enough and then he slowly lowers his head onto his hand, elbow on desk, clicks his pen in and out a bit more and then picks up the request slip, making like to glance at it casually.

Meanwhile Richard has been giving Russ an authoritative stare but when Russ shifts his head onto his hand, Richard lets out a sigh which he probably doesn't want anyone to notice. He lowers his eyes and returns to his desk while Russ and Gail giggle, and so do the guilty by-sitters who obviously just *have* to whisper to each other about how funny the whole thing is.

But what about the hero of this story? It'll be no surprise to you that I cannot see the funny side at all. It's all so unfair and it goes round and round in my head and I'm trying really hard to concentrate on my work but it's so sick and I mean if Richard had asked me to do some of Russ's work in the same situation I'd have done it. Okay I hate the bloke but what's one bit of work compared with another? It's all our work, is it not? Okay I hate the job too, and job satisfaction is only a pipe dream to me, but I'm conscientious, and what's all this fuss about anyway? Russ isn't faithful to his inspector or that precious about his work. It's just an excuse so that he doesn't have to help anybody else. Why couldn't he have just done the work when asked instead of throwing his toys out of the pram and causing all this hurt? Or why did Richard have to ask *him* of all people? Why did I volunteer to take on Dave's work in the first place? Why did I even start working in that nightmare of an office? Why? *Why?*

And while I'm doing myself no good at all with all these whys, the gruesome twosome are whispering and sniggering together and you know how it is when you're in a mood, you think anyone who's whispering and sniggering must be whispering and sniggering about you, but I'm pretty sure that it *is* about me. When I finally finish that bit of work and phone up the guy to give him the information it's really hard to talk to him in a normal voice when the two morons are raising their voices enough so that I can hear, 'The idiot in the corner.' Again. With a gulp I just about manage to say, 'Goodbye, sir,' to the bloke and I put the phone down and give the terrible two a black look and then the phone rings again and the morons giggle again.

'Oh, hullo, yes it's being done. (It's about the quote that Russ is reluctantly doing.) Would you hold on, please and I'll just find out … Russ, have you done that quote?' And the bastard gives me another greasy grin and saunters towards my desk at a snail's pace and throws the piece of paper into the air and it flutters down agonizingly slowly to land at my feet so that I have to bend over to pick it up like I'm bowing to the moron. 'Hullo, yes it's just being typed now. It'll be ready in five minutes. I'm sorry about the wait.' And there's more sniggering as I creep round to the typists' pool where, as it's 4.55pm, everyone is putting their coats on ready to go home. 'Sorry, could someone type this urgent quote please?'

'What? It's too late now. The covers are on the typewriters.'

'Please?'

'It's okay, I'll do it,' says a sympathetic typist.

'Look at his face!' says another.

Giggles all round. I'm hating this place worse than ever by now. Hate the job. Hate the people (some of them). Hate the city. My face must be so black that I've no chance of pretending that it's not black if you know what I mean. I've never been any good at hiding my feelings.

Thanks to the only helpful typist, the quote is out within the remaining five minutes of the day and then when we're all leaving the office I hear Russ say to Gail, 'The idiot in the corner threatened me, did you hear that?' He laughs and of course she laughs too and they whisper to each other again and I know it's about me.

'*I told you! If you've got something to say, say it to me! I'm not kidding!*'

But someone pulls me away and I stomp to the station and I'm fuming and I'm thinking how much I'd like to beat the bastard senseless and watch him writhing on the ground, wallowing in his own blood. Boy, am I really mad! All the way home on the train I can't get the thing out of my mind. What have I done to deserve this? I volunteered to do extra work to save any arguments and so I could work in peace but look what happened. Why all the fuss about one stupid quote? It's the only thing that the manky morons had been asked to do all day and it was the boss who asked them but they had to take it out on me, and all because I needed help and it wasn't even me who asked them but they're convinced that they're in the right and I'm in the wrong and why keep calling me *the idiot in the corner*? Seems to me that they're the ones acting like idiots. Worse than those schoolkids I told you about. No respect or consideration for anyone except themselves. As I've said, some people never learn and some get worse.

I'm so fouled up and depressed. I've been trying to find a different job but jobs are scarce so I'm stuck in that crappy office. I remember when I first started straight from school and I actually thought I'd be happy there. Happy? Huh! I was so naïve then and I guess I was still naïve when I offered to do Dave's work this morning. Maybe there's no place for the innocent in this world, or at least not in the office world. Not in *that* office. That guy in the train was right. 'It's typical though, is it no'? Nae respect fur onybody nowadays.' But *is* it typical? Is that sort of behaviour typical in every office? If not, how did I end up in this one? Are there people like that everywhere? How come I'm so unlucky to be working with them? In my first job? The bastard! I'm going to smash his greasy face in! Never ever have I felt so angry, depressed and miserable all at the same time. What can I do? Can I really smash his face in? It's not my way because I'm not violent but there's only so far I can be pushed. Everyone has a breaking point.

These thoughts run round and round in my head all the way back to town in the train and I keep thinking that I have to find a solution or I'll never get any peace and I'm still thinking that when I'm walking from the station to our house, where Mum and Dad know that there's something wrong because I'm not saying anything and I'm not eating anything either and I'm blacker than a black hole and that's kind of like what it feels like because I'm trapped and I can't get out until I find a way to escape from this storm that's whirling round and round and destroying my life and that's how bad it is, I'm telling you.

So I tell the story to Mum and Dad and after they've heard it they're nearly as angry as me, well not that angry but concerned for sure.

'I'm gonna hit the bastard tomorrow,' I tell them. 'I'll threaten him so bad that he has to fight me. It's the only way I can get this monster off my chest. I've tried to reason with him but the moron won't listen. Yeah, I'll threaten him in the office in front of everyone so that his pride won't let him back down and he won't laugh at me this time!'

'No ye won't,' says Dad. 'That's how you get the sack. Don't be stupid.'

I'm still fuming as I bang and clatter my way up to my room and start kicking furniture around even though I'm pretty quiet most of the time and definitely not violent as I told you before and I don't go around looking for trouble and I try to avoid it without being a coward and sometimes it takes more courage to walk away from provocation rather than rise to it and that's how I try to be but not this time because this is different because I can't work with that fucking bastard until this is sorted out once and for all. In the past I've ignored him or tried to convince myself that when he torments me it's only a joke but this time I'm really mad and I just want to hurt the fucker.

How disgusted with me are you? I told you it's not a nice story, didn't I?

Anyway, Dad comes into my room and he sits down with me on the bed and we have a heart to heart talk and eventually he calms me down and gives me some Really Solid Advice which goes a long way towards solving my problem.

'What you were saying downstairs, son, it's not right, y'know. If you threaten somebody in public it shows a total lack of control. You can't hit him where people can see you, that's a sure fire way of getting the sack. I remember working in an office where this guy hated this other guy and he waited until they were out the back one day and then he hit him. So if you really have to hit him, get him in a close or something, then hit him, okay?'

'Okay, Dad. Thanks.'

'Right, and let me know how you get on.'

'Right, I will. Night, Dad.'

I've forgotten to ask him what happened to those other guys, haven't I? But I feel a bit better after that although I still can't get over the injustice of it all and I go to bed feeling pretty miserable. What if he beats me? He's bigger than me and he's probably been in more fights but I'll still have to fight him because you have to stand up to bullies, don't you? And if I don't I'll never get any peace or have any self-respect, will I? So I toss and turn all night and my sleep (and there's not much of that) is haunted by nightmares of scrapping with the fucking moronic bastard.

Next morning on the train I go over the plan for the umpteenth time. I'm going to get to the office early and wait outside until I see him coming and then push him into the close and threaten him again, only this time he'll get mad because I pushed him and he'll hit me first and then it's a fair fight, y'know, because I want to beat the bastard fairly.

I get on and off the train and if there's any friendly attendants or reluctant ticket inspectors or nosy busybodies or sweaty and stinking smokers or nice views or depressing scenes out of the window or rubbish and muck at the city centre or bored ticket collectors or injured pigeons I don't notice any of them because there's only one fucking thing in my fucking head and that's confronting the fucking bastard that's making my fucking life a fucking misery.

And there he is! Oh no! He's early! He's at the office steps before I get there, and my legs go all shaky and jelly-like and my heart jumps into my throat and I think I can't do it because I can't get him in a close and Dad warned me not to do it in the office but I have to or there'll be no end to it and I'm not going to get through another day and night if

I don't do something *right now!* So I follow him up to the cloakroom and there's nobody else there and my heart's pumping away like mad and I'm shaking all over and I'm scared and I need a shite but I'm trying to focus on everything he's done to make me feel this way and I know that there's only one way to bring an end to it.

He leers at me with that despicable, mocking grin. Even first thing in the morning he looks greasy and slimy. I take a deep breath and look him in the eye and stutter, 'I-I w-wasn't kidding yesterday, Russ.'

'Come on, don't give us that again.'

He's still laughing at me!

I give him a push and that does it because he punches me full in the face and grabs me round the neck and tries to trip me up and then there's a confused shuffling and he's still trying to trip me and all the time his arm's locked round my neck and I'm having trouble staying on my feet and I'm thumping him on the back of his head and his ear and I'm pulling his greasy hair to get at his face and I don't really connect properly but then he's only hit me once and that was the first time and I'm so mad that I haven't even felt it and then we break off as someone comes in to hang up his coat and he's one of the quiet ones and he doesn't say a thing and pretends that he hasn't seen anything.

The whole thing can't have lasted more than ten seconds.

I walk out into the corridor and I must look flushed because the boss's secretary asks me what's going on. 'Oh, nothing,' I say. 'We're just having a laugh.'

She looks at Russ behind me. 'That's right,' he says. 'Just a laugh.'

'Well, as long as that's all it is,' she says doubtfully. She must know that there's more to it but she says no more and walks away and I think we've got away with it and Russ and I walk into the washroom together and he offers me his hand and we shake on it and we're both sort of smiling.

'You admit you were wrong to call me an idiot?'

'A bit.'

And that'll have to do because that's the best I'll get from him. If I was surprised when he offered me his hand, I'm even more surprised now. He picks a bit of fluff off the shoulder of my jacket. This small gesture is more than I hoped for and then we help each other to clean up and he agrees not to annoy me anymore. I never knew that he was capable of so much civility but like me he doesn't want to lose his job.

*

So it wasn't the final showdown like at the end of Western films when the good guy shoots the bad guy and they all live happily ever after. I hadn't beaten him but he stopped annoying me after that. I'm not saying we became buddies. We ignored each other most of the time. The main thing was that the bullying was over and that was all I had wanted.

And that's my story. Did I do the right thing? Maybe. Maybe not.

But it worked.

What would you have done?

As I may have mentioned, when you leave school and go to work in an office, you don't expect people to behave like undisciplined kids. You think they'll be civilised and mature, with respect for others.

But some folk never learn.

Happy Ending

All of his life, Adam was misunderstood. Every time something went wrong, Adam got the blame. Nobody knew the real Adam because nobody ever bothered to find out.

Until that nice lady at the social centre told him about these *mentors* who make sure you're okay. 'They work through your problems with you,' she said. 'It'll be good for you, Adam.'

Adam was nineteen, not a kid any more. It was his last chance to get this kind of help. Okay, he had mild learning difficulties but he was an adult, even if he didn't really understand what *mild* meant and how his *learning difficulties* affected him. He knew what *no fixed abode* meant though, and that he needed to find somewhere to live soon. His girlfriend was going to give birth any day now and she'd need his help, more than most new mothers: she was physically disabled. So, yeah, he had to find a decent place for all three of them to live. He also understood that there was another problem: he'd been accused of sexual abuse.

So, learning difficulties (mild); no fixed abode; sexual abuse accusation; pregnant, disabled girlfriend. Could a mentor sort out all that—get rid of the accusation, find him a place to live, get *custody* (another word he thought he understood), find the real Adam? It was worth a try. Nobody else was going to bother.

*

Bernard, an older and wiser man, Adam's newly appointed mentor, had questions, too. What had happened to make Adam homeless? Where was he sleeping? Where were his parents? What had already been done to find him a home? How much did his learning difficulties affect his understanding? When was the baby due? Were they going to bring it up together or apart? How disabled was his girlfriend? When had the accusation been made? How much was still hanging over Adam, and how would it affect any access to the child? So many questions.

The mentoring agency could provide only some of the answers. Adam and his dad were sofa-surfing at a friend's house. When Adam's mum had died a few years ago, his dad turned to drink, lost his job and lost their house. Father and son were still grieving.

Lizzie, Adam's girlfriend, had stunted growth in both legs and both arms. She could walk only a few metres at a time, more often relying on her wheelchair. She couldn't pick up or hold anything, and was unable to feed herself. She wouldn't be able to hold their baby. She needed full-time care and support, which her foster parents and a team of carers provided. Adam wanted to take the place of the foster parents. Together they could bring up the baby.

Bernard, however, wondered if Adam, after an accusation of sexual abuse, would even be allowed to see the baby.

At that first meeting, the older man's first impressions of his young mentee were: stocky physique; clumsy movements; dark, bushy hair and eyebrows; unkempt, weeks-old beard. Adam, cheerful and unrealistically optimistic, talked enthusiastically about the impending birth. How much he wanted to be a dad and needed to find somewhere to live so that he and Lizzie could bring up their baby together. About his own parents, he said that he missed his mum and needed to get away from his dad. 'He doesn't let me out,' he proclaimed, which clearly wasn't true. Nevertheless, freedom (of sorts) to be a father; to have a place to live, time to grieve, to become a man. He would do anything he could to achieve those goals, and understood that alone he had no chance. Given what he had been told about mentoring, he believed that this was his way forward. And now was the time to grasp the opportunity.

Of the accusation, he said nothing.

However, Bernard had heard the 'official' story. A year ago, two younger boys had been calling Adam names, making fun of his learning difficulties and the way he walked. According to Adam, he'd pushed them against a wall and told them to stop. He'd hardly touched them, just scared them. According to the boys, however, he pushed them into a public toilets and touched them inappropriately. One of the boys tried to describe penetration. When the police questioned Adam, he stuck to his story. 'Prove it,' he challenged them. And when they couldn't, the case was closed. But the accusation remained on his record, which was available to the authorities who would decide on custody of the unborn child; their prime concern was safeguarding.

Bernard saw a vulnerable young person who was about to go through a life-changing ordeal that he couldn't comprehend.

Someone who needed help.

Bernard's help.

However, would Bernard's own resilience be strong enough to support this young man through such colossal challenges?

Adam didn't understand what had happened, was happening or would happen, but Bernard did, and went into the mentoring placement with eyes wide open.

He knew that after the next few months, Adam's life would be altered out of all recognition. Bernard understood that, whatever the outcome, there would be no happy ending. One of Adam's goals was impossible: he would not achieve custody of his soon-to-be-born child. He might not even gain access. It would be part of Bernard's task to let him down gently, to support him through legal hearings and perhaps worse on the way to an inescapable conclusion: Adam would lose his child.

The birth was imminent. Bernard resolved to be at the new dad's side.

*

The baby arrived early, before Bernard and Adam met for a second time. Adam was in the hospital at the time of the birth, but not in the delivery unit. Because the staff had heard about the accusation. However, under close supervision, Adam was later permitted to visit Lizzie and their baby girl, who had been born by Caesarean section because Lizzie wasn't able to push. The baby was small but perfect. They called her Kaylee-Ann.

Bernard first heard of the birth from Lizzie, not Adam, because Lizzie had the phone that she and Adam shared. She asked Bernard to drive Adam to the hospital and bring a change of clothes for her. Sorry, no, Bernard explained, he was a long way from where Adam was sofa-surfing and even further from the hospital. The conversation went nowhere and everywhere. How would the new parents stay in touch with each other with only one phone, and why did Lizzie take it? It would have made more sense for Adam to have it: he was of no fixed abode, and Lizzie could use a hospital phone. And what of Lizzie's abode? Why hadn't she asked her foster parents for help? Surely her clothes were at their house, and more to the point, did they not have a duty of care to their foster child?

Poor Lizzie. Her disability prevented her from holding her own baby. She must have been feeling helpless, excited, scared and unsure where to turn, all at the same time. But, Bernard wondered suspiciously, was she being manipulative? Commandeering the phone, expecting Bernard to drive Adam to and from the hospital to meet her needs, for both to be at her beck and call. Something was not right about the foster home. Did Lizzie see Adam, and for that matter, their baby, as an escape route from her situation, as Adam saw mentoring as a way out of his? Had the pregnancy been an accident, or planned? Bernard knew that the baby would be no escape for Adam, despite his aspirations. But for Lizzie? She couldn't look after the baby on her own, but if she was with Adam, where and how would they live?

Maybe in different circumstances Adam would have been able to help bring up Kaylee-Ann, but everyone except Adam understood that this would not be allowed. Even Lizzie knew, but what else did she know? How far ahead was she thinking? As a new mother, disabled, she could access support from the authorities. Someone must have explained her rights to her. Was that someone putting other ideas into her head?

Was Bernard being unfair? Was he prejudiced against a disabled person? He thought not. Lizzie's disability was obvious for all to see. However, not all disabilities are visible. Adam had one too, however mild. Lizzie had a difficult life and faced huge challenges, but so had Adam.

Lizzie would have access to multiple support agencies.

Adam had Bernard.

Everyone would see Lizzie as the victim, and Adam as the bad guy.

Bernard had to focus on Adam's welfare.

What to do first? Bernard wanted to help Adam come to terms with his feelings while his girlfriend and daughter were in hospital, and afterwards. However, the immediate priority was to help him find somewhere to live, and then explain gently that he'd be living on his own. Adam didn't need to know yet that he would never live with his daughter, but he had to understand that he needed an address that was more permanent than his dad's friend's sofa.

But even before that, mentor and mentee had to find a way to keep in touch, which was simple: Bernard used part of the agency's activity budget to buy Adam a phone. Sitting with him in a shopping centre café, Bernard wondered about Adam's learning difficulties. As Adam's head turned from his new phone to the instructions booklet and back, he was focused. He learned quickly and had the phone set up before he'd finished his drink, much more quickly than Bernard could ever have done.

Now they could maintain contact for the learning, understanding and support that really mattered.

Because Lizzie and Kaylee-Ann were leaving the hospital.

They were going 'home'.

But not to the foster home.

Because the foster parents couldn't cope with a disabled foster child *and* a baby.

So, former foster child and baby were going to move into a temporary care home.

In another city.

A hundred miles away.

*

It was easier to find somewhere for Adam to live than to arrange a visit to his daughter and girlfriend.

Bernard spoke with the manager of a local hostel with live-in staff who supported their vulnerable residents with life skills. There was a vacancy and it was relatively simple to sign the documents and arrange transfer of Adam's housing benefit to the hostel. Within a week, Bernard was collecting Adam from his temporary sofa and helping him to move into his new home a few miles away. As a precaution, Bernard took a colleague with him, in case Adam's dad caused any problems as his son vacated his friend's house. However, far from not letting his son out, he helped him move, and not unkindly. At the point of departure, father and son hugged each other and vowed to keep in touch.

Bernard and his colleague couldn't help but notice how few belongings Adam owned. The hostel would provide cooking utensils, crockery, cutlery and other essentials, but there were personal items such as toiletries and clothes that the agency would source. Which was important, as Adam would soon be making a long journey to visit Kaylee-Ann and Lizzie.

Because, after much negotiation with the care home staff and Kaylee-Ann and Lizzie's social workers, Bernard was going to accompany his mentee by train to visit the two most important girls in his young life.

*

'No thumbs!' Bernard told Adam as he snapped photos at key landmarks between the train station and the care home, such as buildings, road crossings and street signs. Adam insisted on pulling a silly grin and sticking both thumbs up. Provided that the visit to Lizzie and Kaylee-Ann was conducted safely and without incident, Adam would be granted two more visits, which he would have to manage on his own. A pictorial record would be an ideal guide. Adam was enjoying the journey, but without a clear idea where it would really take him.

It was an awkward reunion for the two young people. Obliged to stay in the room, Bernard and a member of the care home staff sat quietly in opposite corners, working on their laptops and pretending not to listen to the stilted conversation between their charges. Which wasn't really a conversation:

it was Lizzie telling Adam what to do and what not to do. The love that Adam felt for Kaylee-Ann was obvious, as he held her in his arms, gazed into her eyes and made soothing noises. Freshly shaven and dressed in smart new clothes, he looked every inch the proud father, trying his best to impress his girlfriend and do the right thing. Perhaps he was also willing the care staff to believe that he could bring up his daughter. Or perhaps, overcome by the emotion of the occasion, he hadn't thought that far ahead.

On the way home, Adam was simply grateful for this opportunity to have spent time with Kaylee-Ann, and for what he described as a good day out. He knew that he was going back home to a hostel. Knew that it was an unsuitable place for a child to grow up. Thought that he would still like to live with Lizzie.

Adam must have made an acceptable impression on the care staff, because the next two visits went ahead as planned. During interim meetings with Bernard, Adam described how Kaylee-Ann was growing up and how proud he felt. He hardly mentioned Lizzie or the care staff. Bernard had heard nothing about any future living arrangements for mother and daughter. Or about access for the father.

Meanwhile, Adam showed Bernard the kitchen in the hostel and offered him a lasagne that he had learned to make in cookery lessons. They played football in the large back garden. They travelled by train to the city museum, and by car to the local seaside resort, where Adam struggled to clamber over the rocks but, deadpan, shunted Bernard's bumper car all over the track on the pier.

As reward for Adam's efforts so far, Bernard took him to watch Adam's favourite football team. Perhaps it was a release of tension that caused the stream of vitriol that poured from the young person's mouth. However, the older man felt obliged to remind him that he was there as reward for his achievements: living semi-independently; adhering to the visits to the care home and his meetings with Bernard; being polite to others; and maintaining dignity in the face of adversity. Yet, here he was, face full of hate, venting his anger upon the other team and their supporters, whose only crime was to wear different colours. What would Lizzie, Kaylee-Ann or the care home staff think if they could see him now? The authorities were about to decide where Kaylee-Ann should live and who would live with her, or visit her. How would they feel if they knew about today? Of course Bernard wasn't going to tell them, but Adam had to learn that good behaviour wasn't only for those occasions when a positive impression was required. He needed to maintain exemplary conduct all the time.

Adam apologised, promised to do better, and was quiet for the remainder of the match. So far, Adam had shown—in equal measures—friendliness, confusion, humility, excitement, gratitude, denial, politeness. But never anger and hate. Until now. Which caused Bernard to wonder if this was the real Adam. Was there some truth in the accusation of sexual abuse of over a year previously? Had Adam been too quick to say *prove it*? Bernard tried to put these thoughts to the back of his mind.

Innocent until proven guilty.

A mantra about to be put under a severe test.

*

Bernard received a call from Kaylee-Ann's social worker, requesting that he accompany Adam on another visit to the care home.

For the registration of the baby's birth.

The young parents travelled from the care home to the register office by separate taxis: Lizzie, Kaylee-Ann and the girls' social workers in one; Adam, Bernard and the care home manager in the other. On arrival, there was a brief discussion that Bernard couldn't hear, then he and Adam were asked to wait in the lobby while all the others entered the room. Strange, thought Bernard, but supposed that they would be called in soon. But no, when the two social workers came out—one pushing Kaylee-Ann in her pram and the other pushing Lizzie in her wheelchair—they walked straight past and into their taxi. Lizzie didn't even look at Adam.

'What just happened in there?' Bernard asked the care home manager as Adam, out of earshot, clambered into the second taxi.

'I'm really sorry,' she replied. 'Lizzie didn't want Adam in the room because she doesn't want his name on the baby's certificate.'

'What? Can she do that? Adam's the father.'

'I'm afraid she can, and she doesn't want Adam to see Kaylee-Ann anymore.'

'Can she do *that*?'

'Apparently so. She's been receiving advice.'

'Advice? Did you know about this?'

'Not until we arrived at the register office. I'm really sorry.'

'But Adam's done everything asked of him. And he's just travelled a hundred miles for the registration of his daughter's birth. Did no one think it mattered to tell him the truth? He has feelings, you know.'

'I can't tell you how sorry I am, and I don't know how to say this any other way, but you and Adam are not to come back to the care home. The taxi has to take you straight to the station.'

How was Bernard going to explain that to Adam?

Nobody said anything in the taxi.

But on the train, Bernard told Adam straight, sticking to the facts.

'Oh well, I still enjoyed the day out,' was all that Adam said.

If only he knew what was coming next.

*

Lizzie, of course, had been listening to her social worker, who arranged a meeting with a solicitor. And Lizzie listened to her, too.

Although Adam didn't have a social worker, he now had free legal representation. His new solicitor knew that Adam had no chance of custody. Their best result would be reasonable access.

Which was about to become almost impossible.

Because Lizzie accused Adam of rape.

She even built a social media hate campaign against him.

The prosecution prepared to cite that Adam, under the influence of alcohol, often became angry and sometimes violent. Bernard had witnessed Adam's anger only once, but had never seen him drink alcohol, nor known him to be under its influence. There was, of course, the previous accusation of sexual abuse, dismissed because of lack of evidence. This time, according to Lizzie, Adam had pushed her in the wheelchair down a deserted lane, lifted her out, laid her on the ground and forced himself on her. She said that she had told him to stop but he wouldn't.

The defence prepared to counter that the two young people had enjoyed sex many times, always consensual. That although Lizzie was physically weak, she was the dominant one in their relationship. The only reason that she made an accusation a year after the incident was to gain sole custody of Kaylee-Ann.

First of all there was a police interview. Bernard would be with Adam as a responsible adult.

Amanda, Adam's solicitor, advised both to say nothing other than 'no comment'.

*

The police officer started the interview by smiling with bright eyes and, in a friendly manner, asking Adam how he and Lizzie got together.

'No comment,' replied Adam.

Bernard, saying nothing, observed Amanda watching proceedings with her trained eye, probably waiting for an opening to pounce, should the police officer give her one.

'What did you two get up to?' the policeman continued, conspiratorially.

'No comment.'

'Lots of kissing?'

'No comment.'

'Cuddling?'

'No comment.'

'Did you have sex?'

'No comment.'

'Hm, and you live in Albion Street, right?'

'No, Albion Avenue, I mean no comment.'

'Oh, Albion Avenue, sorry. And you're eighteen, right?'

'No, nineteen, I mean no comment.'

'Look, this isn't helpful,' said the police officer in exasperation, turning to Amanda, and pointing to Bernard. 'We're not going to get anywhere if *he* just sits there, saying nothing. He's supposed to be a responsible adult.'

'He is,' replied Amanda. 'He and my client are following my instructions.'

'Can I say something?' asked Bernard. 'Adam doesn't know which questions are safe to answer and which ones might be a trap. Do you, Adam?'

'No comment.'

Suddenly, with that (no) comment, the tension was released, they all smiled and agreed amicably to suspend the interview until such time as another approach could be found.

Which, eventually, was this: the police officer didn't believe Lizzie's accusation. He agreed that it was vindictive, purely to get what she wanted. He offered to send his proposed questions to Amanda in advance of the next interview. Promised that if Adam answered them appropriately, there would be no further action taken. Knew that there was going to be more trauma for Adam in the near future. There was no need for him to suffer any longer, not on the police officer's account, anyway. No need for a court case either.

Amanda believed that the officer's motives were sincere. She rehearsed Adam in his replies and eased his anxiety as the second police interview approached.

Which went according to plan, and the case was closed.

Adam was not going to prison.

Now all he had to worry about was the inevitable custody hearings.

And keep off the booze.

Which, spectacularly, he failed to achieve.

*

When Adam missed a mentoring session and stopped answering his phone, Bernard called the hostel to ask if the staff knew anything. He was told that one of the residents had reported money stolen from his room. Coincidentally, Adam suddenly appeared with a crate of lager, inviting everyone to his room to share his haul. When the victim of the theft challenged him, Adam ran away and simply disappeared. It was clear to the hostel staff that Adam had thought that free booze was a good way to forget about his problems and make friends at the same time, and that nobody would know that he stole the money, so that was okay.

If Adam was either unable to predict the consequences of theft or didn't care about them, what chance had he of understanding custody hearings? The first of which was about to take place. Adam had to be there. But Bernard couldn't contact him. Nobody knew where he was. This went on for days.

And then, as suddenly as he had disappeared, Adam picked up Bernard's call. He had been back on his dad's friend's sofa. Although he didn't say as much, he was scared and was waiting for things to cool down before he returned to the hostel.

And now Adam had a greater challenge: if he wanted to see his daughter again, he had to get through the first custody hearing.

*

Reasonable access was what Adam, Amanda and Bernard hoped to achieve.

However, the odds were stacked against Adam: two accusations of sexual misconduct (although neither with a conviction); petty theft and drunkenness (although hardly unique to Adam); failing to attend mentoring sessions and making himself uncontactable (although he came back); learning difficulties (although mild); and living in a hostel (although temporarily). You could forget all the althoughs and all the instances when Adam had been polite, cooperative and grateful. The opposition was looking for reasons *not* to grant Adam custody of his daughter, or even reasonable access. And they hadn't had to look very hard.

Lizzie and her support team knew that the courts usually favour the mother. However, the rape accusation had come to nothing (although muck sticks on the accused); Lizzie had no permanent residence (although the state helps new mothers); she could neither hold nor feed the baby (although she had been living with Kaylee-Ann since the birth); and she couldn't feed or dress herself (although disability support was available). In Lizzie's case, you would *not* forget the althoughs. They would be used to her advantage. Being a victim could work in her favour.

Finally, there was Kaylee-Ann, the centre of it all. Her welfare was, above all else, everyone's primary concern. But what was best for the child could be the saddest news of all for the parents. It was likely that neither parent would win custody or be granted access. In Bernard's opinion, all of the professionals knew what the outcome would be: Kaylee-Ann would be fostered, then adopted. She might never see her birth parents again, unless she chose to find them when she became an adult.

Everyone knew this.

But everyone went through the motions.

Hearing upon hearing.

Legal ramble upon legal ramble.

Tears upon tears.

Until the inevitable happened.

Kaylee-Ann went to live with foster parents in another town.

Two hundred miles away.

Lizzie was housed near the foster home, in supported accommodation.

Adam stayed where he was.

But he was allowed a farewell visit.

*

Adam seemed detached during the long train journey to see his daughter for the final time. He played on his phone, looked out of the window, didn't talk about his feelings. Losing his mother, losing his home, losing his girlfriend, and now losing his daughter. He had come close to losing his freedom twice, the second time because of Lizzie.

While, with absence, Adam and Kaylee-Ann grew further apart than the two hundred miles that separated their temporary homes, Lizzie was living *nearby* and visiting her daughter *every week*. When Bernard had asked why this should be, he was told that Adam was a safeguarding risk to the baby; Lizzie was not.

Maybe this continued contact between mother and daughter was only prolonging the agony, making the final separation even more painful for Lizzie. Kaylee-Ann would not remember, but Lizzie would never forget. Which wasn't Bernard's problem. Adam was.

Bernard looked over at Adam, who was staring out of the window. *What must he be feeling? Does he understand any of this?*

The train pulled into the station, and mentor and mentee, accompanied by a local social worker, made their way to the foster home. Adam showed no emotion. Bernard could have initiated a conversation, which might have helped Adam face this final parting, but decided not to say anything. Sometimes what you don't say is more important than what you do say. Adam would talk when he was ready. Bernard was there for him.

Adam was allowed a full sixty minutes with his daughter, closely supervised, of course.

It was the happiest hour. It was the saddest hour.

Adam was charming to the foster mother, who warmed to him. He asked about Kaylee-Ann's life and if she was happy. The foster mother described their routine, and said yes, she was happy. He commented on the changes in his daughter: how she smiled, the noises she made, the way she moved. She described when Kaylee-Ann first tried to crawl and how she loved to look up into the trees from the pushchair. He took his daughter out for a walk, followed by Bernard and the social worker. She stayed behind, waving to her foster daughter from the door. Just as he would wave goodbye at the end of the hour.

At the end of the sixtieth minute, he cried.

And cried.

He cried in the social worker's car on the way to the station.

He cried on Bernard's shoulder while they waited for the train.

He cried in the carriage.

And, at last, he talked.

Bottled up for so long, his feelings spilled out between gulping sobs.

There was so much he didn't understand. How people could accuse him of things that he hadn't done. Why everyone blamed him. Why his mum had to die. Why his dad drank their home away. Why Lizzie was allowed to see Kaylee-Ann regularly and he wasn't. Why Lizzie suddenly hated him. He talked about all of this.

What he didn't talk about was what happened when he pushed those two boys against a wall, or when he pushed Lizzie in her wheelchair down a deserted lane.

But, finally, he said *this*: 'I want what's best for Kaylee-Ann. If that's adoption, that's that. I'll always love her. I hope we meet when we're older.'

When *we're* older.

They were only children in an adult world.

*

And so the mentoring placement came to an end.

Without a happy ending.

Bernard had helped Adam find a place to live; had provided him with a phone, clothes and other essentials; had accompanied him to court hearings and police interviews and on long journeys to see his daughter; had supported him when the odds were against him; had believed in him, even when Adam had let himself down.

Only at the end of the placement had Adam revealed his true feelings. Perhaps much of what he had said over the months had been denial and fabrication, but in the end his feelings were genuine. Bernard signposted Adam to bereavement support, which he would have to follow up himself; Bernard alerted the hostel staff to keep an eye on his former mentee.

Bernard wondered if he could have done more, and earlier. If he should have applied more pressure on Adam to encourage him to talk. Bernard had wanted to avoid confrontation which, like the stolen money incident, might have scared Adam away. Maybe Bernard should have risked confrontation and possible loss of trust to help a vulnerable young person towards a better life.

It could have been much worse, but Bernard wondered if the end result was no better than damage limitation.

That was the end of the placement.

But not the end of the story.

*

Months later, the baby's social worker contacted the agency. Kaylee-Ann was about to be adopted by a family in an unnamed location. Unlike the foster mother, the adoptive mother did not agree to contact with the birth parents while Kaylee-Ann was a minor. However, there would be a second goodbye, a final farewell from each young parent. Bernard was invited to accompany Adam to the foster home one more time, so that a father could say goodbye.

Again.

Surely that would be cruel, thought Bernard. Adam had already said goodbye, expressed his emotions, and reached a sort of peace. Why prolong the agony?

But Adam was of age. He could make his own decision.

He chose to see his daughter.

*

Bernard collected their tickets at the station, ready for the early morning train.

Waited for Adam at the entrance.

And waited.

Phoned Adam.

No answer.

Ran down to the platform, in case he had missed him.

No Adam.

Ran back up to the entrance.

Still no Adam.

Phoned again.

Still no answer.

Tried the platform again.

The train pulled in.

And left.

They had missed the train to a father's final farewell to his daughter.

The father would never see his daughter again.

Later, Bernard learned that Adam had apparently slept in, and his phone had run out of battery.

But what really happened on the morning that a father missed his last chance to see his child?

What really happened on that day when he pushed his girlfriend in her wheelchair, down a deserted lane?

What really happened when he pushed two boys against a wall?

What

Really

Happened?

*

Two young boys, loitering outside public toilets, with nothing better to do than watch the fat guy with learning difficulties waddling towards them. Maybe he just needs the toilet, they think. Nothing for us to worry about.

Two teenage lads appear from behind the toilet building. 'Oh look, it's Simple Simon,' one of them says.

'My name's Adam,' the guy replies.

'Whatever. What are you doing here, Fat Man?'

'Need a wee,' Adam mumbles.

'What a coincidence,' says the other teenager. 'So do we. We can wee together. Ha-ha, see what I did there?'

Adam looks at them blankly.

'Fancy a drink, Simon? Come on in, we want to show you something.'

The two younger boys stand aside as Adam follows the other two inside. After a while, they peer round the corner and see the three swigging from cans of lager. One of the teenagers stares at them threateningly. The younger boys know that this should be a good time to leave, but curiosity keeps them hanging around outside the door. Who knows, maybe they'll be offered a drink too.

When they hear grunts and then a muffled cry, they can't resist another look. What they see causes them to freeze on the spot. Horrified, they can't tear their eyes away from a scene that makes no sense to them. One of the teenagers sees them, pulls his trousers up and lurches towards them menacingly. They turn to flee but are distracted by the sight of Adam face down in the piss, with his trousers round his ankles, something stuffed in his mouth, and the other teenager crouched on top of him. They don't get away quickly enough and the first teenager catches them and shoves them against the wall.

'Right, kiddies, here's what happened …'

Terrified, the two boys nod in unison, listening without understanding. One of the boys turns to the other in bewilderment. He feels a warm wetness trickle down his legs.

'N-n-no!'

'Y-y-yes! Because if that's not what you say to the police, I'll know. And I know where you live. You get me?'

The two boys nod frantically.

'Now piss off!'

They run away, faster than they've ever run in their short lives.

They don't see the two teenagers leave, laughing and knocking back more lager.

They don't see Adam lying alone in his pool of piss, crying for his mum.

Later, they tell their rehearsed story to the police, who then call on Adam.

'Prove it,' Adam says, but he doesn't tell them the truth.

He's been threatened too.

He doesn't fully understand what happened.

But he feels deep shame.

*

Adam pushes Lizzie in her wheelchair, down a quiet, leafy lane. He loves the peace and quiet here, away from the pandemonium of sofa-surfing at his dad's friend's house. He was helpless when his mum died, then when his dad drank their money and home away, and finally when those two lads lured him into the toilets with their lager and laughter. He can't process the loss of mother, money, home, family life, innocence. He feels he has no control over what happens to him. Except when he's pushing Lizzie in her wheelchair. When he's the one in control. She relies on him.

He thinks that she can help him get some things back. It's too late to return to innocence, he'll never know the love of his mum again, he probably won't know Lizzie's love either. But with Lizzie, he might get some money; he's vaguely aware of support for young couples, especially with a baby. More important than money, they might get a home. The fact that there's no baby isn't the worst of his problems. He's pretty sure he knows how to make one. He's not as dumb as people think he is.

When the lane ends at a secluded patch of woodland, Adam stops pushing the chair, and lifts Lizzie out. He lays her down on a soft blanket of leaves and kisses her clumsily. She kisses him back and smiles. He starts to take her clothes off, and she's still smiling. He drops his trousers and turns her over onto her front. He can't tell if she's smiling now, but she's saying no. He doesn't think she means it. He's heard about girls who say no and mean yes. And it didn't make any difference when he said no in the toilets, did it? They didn't stop then, and he's not going to stop now. He has to go through with this. So does she. It doesn't matter that she can't move her arms or legs; that she can hardly wriggle, even. She doesn't have to do anything. She just has to lie there. He's the one in control. She has to do what he wants. There has to be a baby so that he can have a home and family again.

So that he can have a happy ending.

Wilt

Wilt was unlucky in love.

More accurately he was unlucky in sex. But for his unfortunate nickname he might have been luckier, more firmly endowed and vigorous in his performance. However, nicknames are here for a reason, and Wilt was Wilt in name and wilting in nature.

It all started at primary school when Wilt's sunflowers were the first to bend over. Hardly had they begun to stand up than they collapsed, pathetically spent before their time. Even his pet caterpillars wilted. Wilt was so traumatised as the wiggly beings liquified before his eyes that he would suffer from nightmares for years. His doctor referred him to a mental health specialist. However, the new patient was too disturbed for even the expert to achieve a tangible outcome, other than name a new medical condition: Wilt's Disorder.

As a teenager he tried to spike his hair. It was a flop. Not even the designer Erectorgel worked for droopy Wilt. Then came his fateful entry into a world of fumbling, flaccid sex, or lack of it. Wilt's sex life withered before it had even taken root when his already sagging confidence was flattened after a disastrous first date. Which was made a hundred times worse when Mouthy Martha broadcast his limp performance to anyone and everyone. He hoped that all the hurtful ridicule would fade away but it only stiffened its resolve. He wished that he could do the same.

One of his teachers told him that practice makes perfect, and one of his so-called mates quipped that if he practised with his left hand it felt like somebody else. That's how he came to twiddle away his remaining years at school. It never felt remotely like anybody else but at least his imagination grew.

Finally, school's climactic conclusion arrived. Everyone was dizzy on celebration, with fireworks and feisty flags. Except Wilt, who marked the damp squib of his demise with flagging energy and a subdued soft drink. Alone.

A fresh start was what he needed. Somewhere nobody knew him, where he would be free of his tormentors and could gain confidence at last. Where he could store his energy, hold onto it until the right moment arrived. Only then would he release his spirit and show his detractors what he was made of.

But where was this mythical place, this nirvana of his wet dreams? It would have to be far away from Wiltshire. He might have been less likely to languish in neighbouring Berkshire. Better to be called a berk than Wilt, thought Wilt. Oxfordshire had possibilities. Wilt aspired to be an ox: spirited, strong, stolid, serviceable, stiff and reliably large, especially when full-grown. To cut this long ejaculation short, that's how he ended up studying in Oxford.

Not at the famous university, but in a residential agricultural college, where his withered sunflowers and tortured caterpillars were unheard of and therefore confined to obscure history. Wilt from Wiltshire no longer, he was welcomed as a wholesome, unblemished youth; eager to learn, willing to change. Where they called him …

Will.

Will applied himself at college, and at Young Farmers he learned to socialise. People thought him a bit odd, but oddness was a prerequisite to membership of Young Farmers, so he fitted in quite well. It was there that he met Wilma, a no nonsense farmer's wife-type, churchgoing and potentially censorious. Not perfect then, but she seemed to accept Will. Anyway, he wasn't exactly fighting them off.

When Will and Wilma qualified from college together, all seemed well with their world. Full of respect for each other, they agreed to save themselves until they were married.

That was the beginning of the end for Will.

'The change' came to Wilma earlier than expected. On their honeymoon, in fact. It put her right off the very thought of sex. Which was a huge anti-climax for Will. So unfair. His wife had no respect for his matrimonial rights.

He practised again, but it wasn't the same without Wilma, or so he imagined. She was there but she wasn't there. And when she wasn't there he turned to dirty magazines, but he was too scared that she would be there when he was at it, or discover his hiding place when she was there and he wasn't. So he burned the evidence after every time he pored over it.

Years went by—decades—and Will had to resort to more devious means to ease his still growing frustration. He was approaching old age when he discovered online porn, which was a revelation to Will. He marvelled at the impossible contortions of the actors. Yes, he knew they were actors, that it wasn't real life, but they looked real enough. Surely nothing of Wilma's body was anything like those brazenly displayed on his laptop screen. He saw parts of body parts that he'd never imagined before, probably because Wilma had always insisted on undressing in the dark. He gasped in astonishment at acts that had never entered his dreams. He couldn't believe that they were even legal, and he wondered if he was breaking the law by watching them.

He snapped his laptop shut and wiped himself. As an afterthought he opened his laptop again and wiped it too. Then closed it again. At least Wilma would never find out. She never came into his room. Even if she did, she knew nothing about computers. Or so he assumed; it had been a long time since they had had a meaningful conversation. The truth was, what Wilma did or how she felt were also afterthoughts to Will. He had as much interest in Wilma's activities or feelings as, he surmised, she had about his.

At this point he started to get bombarded with spam emails inviting him to have sex with women living fewer than five miles away, which he suspected was untrue because there were only about a dozen houses within a five mile radius of the farm.

'Our bodies are so drawn together! It's magic!'

'I need to get closer to you tonight!'

'Hey, it's me! Do you wanna see my hot pix?'

'I really feel the need to be with you!'

'I know what u're thinking! It's dirty! U're naughty!'

God! Help! It was all getting too much for Will. He was momentarily tempted but he wasn't a complete imbecile: he knew not to click the links. He'd heard about these tricks to infect your computer. They were certainly infectious but you couldn't get a sexually transmitted disease from a dirty screen, or from your hand, could you? Besides, he wasn't actually going to do anything. He didn't have the nerve to approach a lady of the night.

Oh well, at least what Will did on his own was only a harmless bit of good, clean fun. Well, not exactly clean, but he wasn't hurting anyone. Certainly not Wilma.

Nobody told him about search histories.

Or that Wilma had been attending an IT for the Terrified course.

Will was undone.

Wilma knew exactly what Will had been up to. The upshot was that she threw him out and left him with nothing. She even confiscated his laptop. 'Before the police do,' she said. He didn't think that was true because he hadn't committed a crime. However, she pointed out that all those actors were being exploited; the public were always being asked to report any suspicion of modern slavery.

Will couldn't take the risk of further exposure, so he gave up his laptop and crawled away, defeated, to a deserted shack hidden in nearby, lonely woods, where for years he had been furtively stashing his secret supply of finest, strongest farmer's mead.

Alone again, he thought back to his childhood and teenage years. Everyone calling him Wilt. The nonstop torture. When he promised himself that he would get his own back somehow, someday.

After school he had made a fresh start, gained acceptance, got through college okay, married, achieved moderate success at farming. Mouthy Martha and the rest of his tormentors knew nothing of that. He didn't think they would be impressed even if they knew. Will needed to harden his ambition and rise up to higher expectations, if only to appease himself.

Despite his former nickname, the only thing Will had left was an urge. Which was no good at all. He had no money, no woman, not even the internet. He had a hand in his own downfall, that was all. If only he could be granted three wishes … But that only happened in stories. So, in the time-honoured tradition of a lonely-old-man-caught-watching-internet-porn, he disappeared into a bottle of potent mead. And that's where he stayed for days and nights, haunted by nightmares of a childhood of disturbance, an adolescence of embarrassment, an adulthood of rejection, an old age of disclosure, and a genie.

Wait, stop! *A genie?*

Will knew that he was still drunk, but he wasn't sure if he was dreaming, or awake and hallucinating. He rubbed his eyes and stared down at the pile of empty mead bottles; at blue smoke emerging from the mouth of one of them; growing up into a red waistband; a green jacket failing to hide straining, bulging chest muscles; muscular arms adorned with golden bands and ending with manicured hands, one enclosed in a fist, the other pointing at Will then curling back its fingers invitingly; a too-large head with a pointed black beard, pointed ears and pointed nose; an impossibly huge grin with white teeth shining bright; sparkling blue eyes under pink eyeshadow; high-arched black eyebrows and a purple turban, golden clasp and white feather. So much colour penetrating Will's dark world.

Will failed to clear his throat and rasped impotently, 'This can't be happening.'

'OH YES IT CAN,' boomed the genie, a flurry of blue smoke spouting from his inordinately wide mouth.

'But, how?'

'*HOW* DID I GET HERE? WRONG QUESTION. THE RIGHT QUESTION IS: *WHAT* CAN I DO FOR YOU? BECAUSE YOU ARE IN A BIT OF A MESS, ARE YOU NOT, WILL? LET ME HELP YOU RISE FROM THE DEPTHS OF YOUR DEMISE.'

This got Will's attention. This smoking, swaying, sonorous being, ineffably interfering with Will's consciousness.

'Eh?' Will said.

'EH?' the genie snorted. 'EH! I SHALL TELL YOU WHAT IS *EH*. I AM GOING TO ANSWER YOUR HEART'S DESIRES.'

'Eh?'

'IS THAT REALLY ALL YOU AMOUNT TO? EH? LET ME ENLIGHTEN YOU. YOUR HEART'S DESIRE IS TO HAVE SEX WITH SOMEONE ELSE WITHOUT HAVING TO WORRY ABOUT YOUR PERFORMANCE OR ANYONE FINDING OUT, RIGHT?'

'Erm …'

'OR WHAT YOU LOOK LIKE.'

'Eh?'

'I MEAN, LOOK AT YOURSELF: YOU ARE LIMP, SOFT, SMELLY, AND AS FOR THE REST OF YOU: YOU ARE UNFASHIONABLE, SCRUFFY, HUNCHED, BALD, YOU HAVE FALSE TEETH, YOU HAVE TO WEAR PADS TO PREVENT YOU FROM WETTING YOURSELF, YOU FART A LOT, YOU ARE WELL PAST YOUR PRIME. BUT DO NOT BE CRESTFALLEN: I CAN HELP YOU WITH ALL THAT.'

'Eh?' said Wilt, crestfallen. 'How?'

'I SHALL TELL YOU HOW: APART FROM INCREASING YOUR RANGE OF VOCABULARY, I CAN RETURN YOU TO YOUR PRIME. ACTUALLY, LET US MAKE THAT *BETTER* THAN YOUR PRIME. I CAN RESTORE YOUR YOUTH *AND* INSTALL INSIDE YOU A VIGOUR WHICH YOU HAVE NEVER BEFORE EXPERIENCED. I CAN TURN YOU INTO THE MOST DESIRABLE MALE OF THIS OR ANY CENTURY. I CAN SET YOU UP WITH A HOT DATE WHO CANNOT POSSIBLY TURN YOU DOWN.'

'Eh? How?'

'I CAN STOP YOU REPEATING YOURSELF AND INTRODUCE YOU

TO AN UNBELIEVABLE AND UNFORGETTABLE NIGHT OF PASSION. I CAN HELP YOU TO FULFIL YOUR MOST FANTASTIC FANTASY.'

Will wondered how on Earth this genius of a genie knew exactly what he wanted. Or how, when and where it was going to happen.

'YOU ARE WONDERING HOW, WHEN AND WHERE, ARE YOU NOT?'

'Erm …'

'*HOW?* LEAVE THAT TO ME. *WHEN?* IN A FEW MINUTES' TIME. *WHERE?* RIGHT HERE. I SHALL LEAVE THE *WHAT* TO YOUR IMAGINATION.'

Now. Here. Will would never be ready in time. However, he had just been told to leave the *how*, the *when* and *where* to the genie and the *what* to his own imagination. Ah, yes: the *what*. The absurdity of the situation washed over Will's befuddled mind. If he trusted the genie he would finally have what he had always wanted: vigorous, energetic, long-lasting, powerful, fulfilling, passionate sex. Not only with someone else but with the epitome of his ultimate fantasy.

His imagination swirled in a muddle of mouth-watering anticipation. He wanted her to arrive in a nurse's uniform and black lacy bra, stockings and suspenders. And high heels, it had to be high heels. Legs up to her armpits and big boobs. Long black hair. Seductive eyes thick with dusky makeup, smiling at him enticingly with red, luscious lips. He fantasied further about her revealing all—and in the light, so that he could look at it. Performing the same bodacious contortions that he had seen online. A *whole night* of sexual exultation. Could he keep up?

Of course he could: he would be young, hunky, virile, upstanding and outstanding.

But it was too good to be true. What was the catch?

'YOU ARE WONDERING ABOUT THE CATCH, ARE YOU NOT?'

'Well …'

'THE CATCH IS THIS: THERE ARE THREE CONDITIONS.'

'Oh?'

'ONE: NO MATTER WHO RINGS THE DOORBELL, LET THEM IN AND STAY WHERE YOU ARE.'

'Okay.'

'TWO: AT MIDNIGHT, YOU WILL SHRIVEL UP AND ADOPT YOUR FORMER—OR SHOULD I SAY PRESENT—STATE. SO MAKE THE

MOST OF YOUR TEMPORARY MACHO MASCULINITY.'

Will looked at the old clock on the wall, which on cue chimed three times. 3pm: nine hours of unbridled passion awaited him. Nine hours more than he had ever had in his whole life.

'Okay,' he said.

'THREE: I WANT YOU TO GIVE ME A FIVE STAR REVIEW ON TRIPADVISER.'

'Okay.'

'AND NOW, LET THE SHOW BEGIN.'

The genie disappeared in a puff of blue smoke.

Minutes passed.

More minutes passed.

By then Will believed that it had all been a figment of his imagination. He was going to wake up soon. He knew it was too good to be true.

Then he heard a rumbling from deep within himself. He felt sick and his joints began to ache. Oh no, not another desperate rush to the toilet. Not now!

But it wasn't that. This felt different than his usual intestinal troubles. Something was moving under his baggy clothes. Painful, like his insides were about to burst out of his skin. His arms, torso and legs stretched and strained. Agonisingly, he collapsed to the floor as his buttons popped open, revealing a glimpse of musculature never before witnessed except in porn videos. His scruffy clothes ripped apart, to be replaced by fashionable, stylish wear previously seen only on adverts in his dirty magazines. The pain shifted to his head as thousands of needles pierced his scalp, and his face rippled in waves of affliction. Then, most excruciating of all, he almost fainted from a torturous throbbing in his groin, far worse than the vasectomy that, in the early years of his marriage, Wilma had forced on him—a pointless cruelty because the chances of Will impregnating Wilma were about as remote as him becoming Mister Universe.

Suddenly the pain subsided. A relieved and reborn Will rose to his feet, stumbled in the dark to the window and hauled open the curtains. He blinked at a light unseen for days and staggered across to the mirror. Where he blinked again and stared.

At an apparition of insuperable manliness.

Standing erect before Will was a perfect example of God's gift to manhood. Chiselled chin, high cheekbones, piercing blue eyes, floppy hair (the only thing floppy about the phantasm looking back at him). Will tossed his hair to one side experimentally, and the image did the same. He pulled his lips back in a sort of grimace, and the reflection grimaced back, and then grinned widely, displaying immaculate teeth. He ran his hands over a silk shirt and felt a hardness underneath, which enticed him to undo the buttons and gaze in wonder at a classic six-pack. *His* classic six-pack. Mister Universe. He felt firm buttocks and long slim legs inside a brand-new pair of chinos. Hesitated at an impressive bulge in his crotch. *This* he had to see.

He pulled down the zip, pushed the chinos and designer briefs to the floor and gaped open-mouthed in wonder.

Good God!

The doorbell rang.

No matter who rings the doorbell, let them in and stay where you are, the genie had told him.

Okay.

'Come in!'

The door creaked open slowly and a woman stepped over the threshold. Not in a nurse's uniform, but a police officer's.

Will groaned. So this was the real catch. Caught with his pants down, his nine hours of fervour over before they had even begun. His unfamiliar broad shoulders drooped as his excitement dwindled and he began to resign himself to his more accustomed deflation.

'Stay where you are!' said the police officer as she sashayed into the room, threw off her cap and unleashed a delicious expanse of raven-black hair which framed her face and curled tantalisingly around the twin peaks of her tight uniform blouse. A twinkling eye peered from behind the black screen and winked alluringly.

'Well, *hello*, handsome,' she said huskily as she undid the buttons of her blouse, exposing a black lacy bra barely containing a cleavage heaving to break free. 'You've been a very naughty boy.'

Will's outlook suddenly improved. He pulled his shoulders back and stood tall, painfully aware of his arousal.

She paused from undressing herself and looked down, gawking, eyes wide open, shocked, red lips framing a dramatic 'O'.

'Mmmhmmm, Big Boy. What are we waiting for?'

Will's nine hours of debauchery lived up to every one of his wildest fantasies. Again and again he rose to the occasion, as did his police escort. His climaxes—of which there were multiple—were maintained for inconceivable durations in a feat of remarkable endurance. With each cataclysmic watershed—when it seemed that this must be his final breaking point—he rested only momentarily and then once more into the breach he plunged.

Later, he sheltered happily in the calm before the storm. After a brief doze he rolled towards his delectable but drained companion, and smiled

'Not again?' she croaked, flat-out on the floor, struggling to speak, never mind satisfy her voracious partner's extreme demands.

'I suppose we could wait a *few* minutes longer,' he replied considerately.

During those few minutes Will reflected that this night was the most perfect of his entire life, although, truth be told, there hadn't been much competition. But he didn't care. This was the best feeling ever. At last, after a dull existence of profound disappointment, Will had achieved more than he ever thought possible. Not a dream or a booze-addled hallucination. It was heaven. He could rest now, secure in the memory of his fulfilment in which he finally became the man he always aspired and deserved to be.

His mind drifted back to the shrivelled sunflowers and crumpled caterpillars that spawned years of ridicule. Mouthy Martha's 'kiss and tell' cruelly extending his torture.

Wilma forever denying him of his manly needs. (At least she didn't call him 'Wilt'.) It mattered not that none of them was here to witness his triumph against all odds. He knew what had come to pass on this mountainous, historic night. Nothing else mattered. He could die happy.

But before that, back to the business in hand. He rolled over and nudged his snoring partner, who groaned again and slowly opened her eyes. He raised his manly eyebrows expectantly.

The doorbell rang again.

No matter who rings the doorbell, let them in, the genie had told him.

'Come in!'

Another policewoman entered.

'Perfect!' said Will. 'Your colleague is clapped-out. Come over here, baby.'

He moved towards her, arms open.

Stay where you are, the genie had said.

'Stay where you are!' said the new policewoman, whipping out her truncheon.

'Ooh, that's impressive,' stated Will, 'but not as impressive as … this!'

'Put it away!' she shouted.

Then several things happened at once. The policewoman raised her truncheon above her head; the old clock began to chime again; Will felt ill, overcome by a sinking feeling; the door creaked again; and Wilma marched in.

The clock struck again, and again. Will's whole body began to ache, and he felt himself sagging, shrinking. The clock kept on chiming and when Will glanced over, he saw both hands creep towards the twelve. He had completely lost track of time. He looked down at the floor and saw—not the gorgeous girl of his dreams—but an old, shrivelled woman, peering with bloodshot eyes through stringy, lifeless hair; pouting grotesquely then opening her gap-toothed mouth wide to say, 'Give ush a kish.'

Will doubled over, retching, as the clock struck twelve. He didn't need to look in the mirror to know what he had become. *Wilt* collapsed face-down into a pool of vomit.

'Eeyuch!' said Wilma.

'I am arresting you on suspicion of exploitation,' said the policewoman. 'You have the right to remain silent …'

She helped Wilt to his feet and clapped him in handcuffs, then placed a hand under his elbow and led him towards the door.

'How did you know?' Wilt asked helplessly, turning to Wilma.

'How did I know?' she sneered. 'Oh, I know everything about you and your dirty little secrets, *Wilt.* Your smutty magazines, your secret stash of lethal mead, your lonely hideout. It's amazing what you can find out from somebody's laptop.'

'But I wasn't doing anybody any harm,' pleaded Will. 'You kept shutting me out, even on our honeymoon. What else was I supposed to do?'

'What else!' she exploded. 'You could have understood how I felt, how I still feel. I'm ill! I've always been ill. And what do you do? Ignore me, shut yourself in your room and play with yourself. Poor Wilt. It's all about you, isn't it? It's always been about you. You just don't get it, do you?'

'I do now,' sniggered Wilt.

'You… WANKER!'

'Okay, that's enough,' said the policewoman as she bustled Will out the door. She turned to indicate the old woman on the floor and asked Wilma, 'What shall we do with her?'

'Mouthy Martha? I'll see she's alright,' said Wilma, winking at Will.

God! Can this night get any worse? thought Will as the wind howled and hard rain spurted against his wrinkled old face. He squinted through swirling clouds at a faint wisp of blue smoke in the distance. Amidst the noise of the gathering storm he heard a faint reprise:

'DON'T FORGET TO GIVE ME A FIVE STAR REVIEW ON TRIPADVISER.'

Razorblade Sky

She is nearing the end of her probationary year as a teacher, but only beginning her long run across the moor. She needs this run, not to clear her head—that's never going to happen—but to put her in a more positive frame of mind. Eventually. Hence the *long* run. A short jog round the block wouldn't cut it. Wouldn't even scratch the surface. She needs miles and miles of running after the day she's had. After the year she's had.

Her mind is so full of frustration that it's going to take four or five miles of her planned eleven to shake off her negative, all-consuming thoughts. She knows that by the big hill at mile six she'll leave some of her negativity behind as she climbs out of the depths of despair. As she tops the summit, there will be a shift of perspective and cadence. She will hurtle down the other side, she'll relax and enjoy the second half of the run. She'll feel much better in herself at the finish. If only temporarily.

She knows this because she's done it all before. Running works. It's worked for her all year, and today it has to be eleven miles. One for each of the eleven months it's taken her to get this far. During which her mileage and love of running have increased in inverse proportion to her growing disillusionment with teaching. Her energy to run more miles has developed as her physical and mental strength for teaching has dissipated. Running tires her but also invigorates her. A paradox unravelled every time she runs and recovers, fitter and stronger. Whereas she never recovers from the trauma of teaching. Like a cancer it eats into her, masticating on the remains of another demoralizing day at school.

This malignance has to be endured on the run before her recovery begins. It's tempting to get the first few miles over with quickly, hammer herself, a form of self-harm. Not that she needs to run to self-harm: any number of items in her bathroom cabinet could nudge her towards that end. No, the opening miles are a means to an alternative end, not an end to running, which they might be if early over-exuberance led to injury. Because she knows this, she does not succumb to temptation. She starts slowly as she leaves her front door, crosses the street to a footpath branching out onto the open moor. Leading her to deliverance.

She lets the venting commence.

Four years of teacher training. Of study, excitement, anticipation, promise. For what? Over-fatigue, lassitude, debilitation. Not the temporary tiredness of relatively short teaching practices at university followed by the relief of a return to normal, student life. But a permanent, disabling exhaustion. Teaching itself—mostly a privilege—is draining enough. But everything else—preparation, marking, reports, parents' evenings, late nights, early mornings, pressure from headteacher and governors, league tables, inspections—blend into a poisonous cocktail that melts her down. Until she is too tired to think straight, to take pleasure in her work, to feel privileged, to teach well. To function. At all.

Disturbance, desperation, despondency, depression, desolation, dejection never leave her. Swirling round and round in her semiconsciousness, keeping her awake at night. Even when she falls into a semblance of slumber it's there: a nightmare puzzle that she will never solve, but in her episodic sleep she tries. If only she could find a solution, she could rest in peace.

However, every night ends abruptly with a cacophonous alarm, bullying her into dragging herself out of bed on a morning that comes too soon.

It is no wonder that earlier today, head still in a fog as she arrived at the school gates, she was not on top form. No surprise that she screamed in the classroom after the final straw that broke her back. The details don't matter. What matters is that her spirit was—is—broken.

It is understandable that she fled from the classroom to the headteacher's office in search of support, and when none was forthcoming, to collapse into a hunched, swaying, rocking, hopelessly sobbing heap of a former human being.

Sent home early for once, now on the run, loping along, seeking empathy from her running haven.

The first three miles don't help. It's all she can do not to stop and cry. Or lift her eyes and arms to the sky and plead for salvation.

But she does not stop. She winds between gorse bushes, skitters down stoney paths, leaps over streams. Begins to notice birds singing their hearts out in an attempt to lift her spirits; sunlight peeking out from clouds in an endless sky, trying its utmost to brighten her day; the fresh smell of earth, an antidote to the staleness of school corridors; the cooling breeze on her cheeks, drying her tears; the springiness of the turf, sending energy through her feet and up to her soul.

Sent home early. It's a message. She is long past the stage of not wanting to waste her years of training. Better that than waste her life. She has long ago extricated herself from financial worry. Her parents will help until something turns up.

As she reaches mile six and begins the climb to the highest point of the route, she starts to believe in herself. She lifts her knees, drives with her arms, pushes herself into an entirely different kind of tiredness. The kind that ends in success, not failure. Heart thumping; breathing elevated, rasping, noisy; she breaches the summit and touches an open sky.

And reaches a decision.

She is not going back.

She runs along the top of the crest, her strides become longer, her breathing and heart rate slowing down a little. She has five more miles of running to enjoy as opposed to five more days of the school year to endure. She will enjoy the miles but will not endure the days. She will call in sick. She will break her contract. Cut her ties. She will be free.

Decision made, she breezes across the rocky top and begins to float downhill. Every stride is pure pleasure. She can't put a foot wrong.

*

He staggers over the bumpy moss, heavy camera hoisted across his back. More in hope than expectation, he trudges towards a likely vantage point. Up there, a rocky outcrop. Should be able to see for miles. Search for something worth photographing.

His fledgeling photography business is not a roaring success. He had a few commissions early on. Cute babies cradled by adoring parents. The odd puppy or kitten, even cuter. But no flood of recommendations arrived, no clamouring for his services. The work dried up. So here he is on the open moor, trying his hand at wildlife photography. Although he knows hardly anything about photography and even less about wildlife.

He only tried to make a living out of taking photos because he got a camera as a birthday present. He used to be a typical 'could do better' student, and has not improved. He's too lazy to apply for a job. He has not even walked into the wild: he drove way past the 'no entry' signs, parked where cars are not allowed, and stumbled no more than a hundred metres to this point, where he squints wistfully at the top of the hill in the distance, but stares realistically at a small copse of trees in the foreground. He smiles and thinks, Who wants to kill themselves hiking all the way up there when you can probably get an artistic shot down here, through the branches, pointing *towards* the hill?

The first subject of his new line of work is probably going to be a rabbit or some sort of bird, maybe a deer. He hasn't a clue. He just hopes it arrives soon so that he can get back to the comfort of his car.

Luckily for him it's not long before his first centrepiece appears over the top of the hill, silhouetted razor-sharp against the bright sky. And it's not what he expected. It's a runner. A woman.

She bounds effortlessly down the slope, long legs striding out, arms raised at her sides, perfectly balanced. Free yet vulnerable. Eyes to the ground slightly ahead, long ponytail bobbing behind. She's wearing a simple T-shirt and shorts, exposing elongated limbs. Sex on legs. Like a model.

Fingers fumbling, he begins to snap away. These photos are going to be brilliant. Wait … *like a model.*

He has to speak to her. Stop her. He runs out—waving, shouting—straight into her path.

*

Focusing on where to put her feet, she is aware of a sharp light in her peripheral vision. She thinks nothing of it. Only a reflection of sunlight, probably a piece of glass.

As the ground levels off, she picks up her pace and runs towards a copse of trees. Where a figure leaps out in front of her, blocking her path. She is aware of her vulnerability, miles from anywhere, alone. Instincts kicking in, she swerves, accelerates, sprints away from harm's way.

The danger already outrun, she risks a glance behind. At a man, waving his arms, shouting 'Stop!'

He's going to hurt me, or worse, she thinks. Or he could be lost or injured. Maybe someone else is injured, perhaps a child, and they need help. Her hesitation and glimpse to the rear cause her to lose balance. Instantly her gaze switches back to the front but it's too late: she can't avoid the rock. She stumbles, thuds into it, twists her knee, and something sharp scratches her hand. Weirdly, her next thought is, That's too sharp to be a rock.

And then the pain hits her.

Intuitively she grabs her knee to relieve the hurt. She pulls her hand away and holds it in front of her face. Stares at blood seeping from a narrow slit. Something on the ground glints in the strong sunlight—a blade of some sort?

She hardly has time to think, How did that get here? when urgent footsteps approach.

It's him. He might be coming to her aid or … She tries to struggle to her feet but her leg won't work properly and the pain *moves.* 'OW!' The ground shifts and the sky spins, her eyes roll into the back of her head and everything goes dark.

*

He's pulled off his socks, tied one around her knee and the other across her hand. Now that he's managed to stem the flow of blood, he's laid her on her back, taken off his shirt and bundled it under her head. He would loosen her clothing but there's nothing much to loosen. He needs to get her to his car. She's coming to, muttering something about school, running home, and a blade. She opens her eyes and looks up into his face.

And screams.

*

Something is blocking the sky. A man, on top of her. *Him.*

She screams.

'Get off me!'

She tries to writhe from under him but the agony in her knee and hand slices into her panicked awareness. She's in danger.

'Leave me alone! HELP!'

'Hey,' he says. 'It's okay, I'm here to help.'

'But the blade. Did you—?'

'What blade? Forget that, let's get you to my car. We need to go to hospital. Need to get those cuts checked out.'

'I'm not going anywhere with you!'

'Look, I'm not a weirdo. I'm only trying to help. Besides, what choice have you got? You can't walk, there's no phone signal—I've tried—my car's just over there. Let me carry you. Trust me.'

'I, I—'

'Look at this face: does it not look honest to you?'

She passes out again.

*

He watches her sleeping fitfully. Twitching, squirming, eyelids fluttering. Troubled. In pain.

Like years ago on the moor when they first met.

When she had no choice but to collapse into his manly arms, trust him, rely on him, let him look after her, help her on her way, make decisions for her.

It's been that way ever since.

He made it all happen. It was easy to win her over. Carry her to his car, make her comfortable in her unconsciousness, reassure her as she woke up en route to hospital, strike up a conversation, charm her. In the waiting area, point out how alike they were. Each looking for a change, she from a stressful first year in the classroom, he from a failed start as a photographer. The premature end to her teaching career and the doctor's recommendation that she didn't run for a while to let wounds heal left her with a huge gap in her life. He jumped right in there.

He had always been good at this: manipulating people. He had learned how to do it at school, getting younger children to trust him and do his dirty work for him and then get the blame when it went wrong. Later, egging his mates to perform laddish pranks after the pub, then hiding and leaving them to take the rap when the police arrived.

He was a comfort to her, boosting her self-esteem, seducing her into believing that she had potential as a sportswear model. Luring her into his makeshift studio and then into his bed. Persuading her that it was unwise to return to running, that the injury was more serious than she made out.

He wanted her all to himself.

They weren't making much money, so he persuaded her to ask the Bank of Mum and Dad. Easy as taking sweets from a baby. The next step was to convince her to pose in glamourous clothes, then clothes that left little to the imagination, then no clothes at all.

He knew as much about sportswear or glamour modelling as he did about family or wildlife photography, but he had contacts. Who enlightened him. He could get more for himself by *not* having her all to himself.

It should have taken years and more than boyish charm to brainwash her into sharing her favours with his associates. In the end, all it took was a regular dose of drugs to slide her into a woozy compliance. That's when he started to make some serious cash. He cleaned up.

But now, watching her lying naked on his bed, he knows it's time for another change. Because *she* has changed. He remembers the lithe, slender figure bounding down the hill to fall at his feet. He had stared at her lying on the ground then. Flat tummy, unblemished skin, ponytail splayed out, bright eyes snapping open.

He looks at her now. Podgy, blotchy, more cellulite than sexuality, lifeless hair matted across bags under her eyes.

She'll have to go.

First of all he needs to pop out for fags. That should give the lazy cow time to wake up from her stupor. Then he'll tell her that her time is up. She's served her purpose. He doesn't need her any more.

He closes the bedroom door quietly behind him.

*

Her eyes snap open as she hears the door click shut.

It's time for another change.

He'll have to go.

She knows what he's been doing to her.

*

In the beginning she had believed that he understood how she felt. He rescued her. He supported her decision to cut ties and leave teaching, even though she had no idea what to do instead.

At first it had been fun. Posing in sportswear made her feel good, even in skimpy gear that she would never have dared to wear on a run: a crop top and shorts that were more like bikini bottoms. He had said something like: 'If you've got it, flaunt it. It's good for your confidence.'

Despite the double trauma of the end of her teaching career and the accident on the moor, she had felt in control of her own decisions. Thanks to her mum and dad she didn't have to worry about money, although they worried about how much their daughter was relying on a new boyfriend who had suddenly turned up out of the blue.

Over the years she metamorphosed from posing in sportswear into poisoning her morals and selling her body. Something went awry with her reasoning during those years. She had no idea how it had happened.

However, she started to realise one morning when she awoke from her usual fog, staggered to the window and saw nothing but more fog. She thought she was still asleep but no, it was real fog, which was beginning to lift. As the shutter rose it revealed a blue sky streaked with elongated, jagged clouds, like the pattern in the middle of a razor blade.

She wandered into the bathroom and opened the cabinet. Plasters, pills, bandages, an open razor. He preferred that to a razor blade.

Distant memories pierced her personal fog that morning, cutting through her indifference. She struggled to concentrate. Wondered why she was staring at pills. She knew that they could make you better. They could also make you dependent, and they could alter your perception. *They could change who you are.* Straining to focus, she tried to remember. She hadn't been taking pills, but she had been acting like a different person. As she reeled within her narcosis, a spark leapt out of the ashes of her recollections. *If she didn't take pills, then* he …

He must have been spiking her food or drink. That's how he had bled her dry of integrity.

He always prepared their meals, pretending that he knew something about cooking. In her meek and grateful state, she always let him do it. He used to watch her eat and drink, until one day he had ceased to sit at the table with her, sloping off to flop in front of the TV instead.

After that morning when realisation began to pierce her befuddlement, it was easy to tip her food into the bin and pour her drink down the plughole while he was out of the room, then eat something else when he wasn't in the house. Day by day, she became more lucid, her memories clearer. Including those about bandages, plasters … and razors.

Until she remembered everything. How he had controlled her every decision, every move, every thought.

She hid her discovery from him, pretended that there was no change, went through the motions. Which, in her new consciousness, sickened her.

But not for much longer.

*

Now, lying naked on the bed after the door clicks shut, she knows that the time to confront him is *now*. She can't just sneak out and run away. That would feel like he was still controlling her. No, she'll show him how strong she is.

One way or another,
today
it ends.

*

He clumps up the stairs and sees her standing in front of the open bathroom cabinet. Wonders what she's doing there. She looks different. Still a bit podgy but almost sexy, squeezed into the old running gear that she used to pose in for him. He didn't know she'd kept it. She's still a bit baggy under the eyes but passable, with her makeup carefully applied and hair tied back in a ponytail, like before. Oh well, it doesn't matter, he'll get rid of her anyway. Then again, he could humour her for a bit. She might be good for one last dance.

She sees him leering at her from the top of the stairs. Looks at him as if for the first time and sees him as he really is. Suppresses a gag and wonders how she could have been so easily fooled for so long. *But not anymore.*

The flickering landing lightbulb illuminates his receding hairline and double-chin while sunlight from the bathroom window highlights a new resoluteness on her face.

Each sees the other in a different light.

'Wow! You've still got it, lover!' he says. 'What you doing in that knock-out gear anyway?'

'I'm going for a run.'

'What? Remember what the doctor said.'

'That was years ago.'

'Well, yeah, but it was good advice then and it's good advice now. You don't want to harm yourself, do you?' He opens his arms wide and moves towards her. 'Come here and give me a hug.'

'I'm not going anywhere with you,' she says, pushing him away.

'Don't be like that. Have I not always looked after you? Look at this face: does it not look honest to you? Don't go for a run. Stay here with me. We're good together.'

'I'm going for a run,' she insists, 'after I've dealt with you.'

'What do you mean: dealt with me? We deal with things together. Always have done.'

'No we don't. *You* do. I *know*.'

'What does that mean: you *know*?'

'I know what you've been doing. It's called *coercion*.'

Her eyes hide her fear and her words are firm. She has to go through with this. Otherwise she'll never be free of him.

His eyes flicker with uncertainty. If she really knows, he could be in big trouble. But he might be able to bluff his way out of this.

'You've been talking to Mummy and Daddy, haven't you? You know they've never liked me. They don't understand what we've got.'

'They do now. And before I *go for a run*, I want you to hear this: coercion is a crime. I'm going to report you. And don't try to stop me. *Mummy and Daddy* know where I am and what I'm doing.'

'Come on, lover, you don't want to do that to me. Not after everything I've done for you. Who saved your life on the moor? Who picked you up when you were down? Who gave you a new career?'

'Who *pimped* me, more like!'

'It wasn't like that! All I did was make the best of your talents. You didn't know what you were doing. You needed me to be in control.'

He sees her staring back at him, unmoving, and he changes tack.

'You're nothing without me!' he spits. 'I mean, look at yourself now. Gone to seed. Forget what I said earlier: you haven't still got it. You're a joke, bulging out of that skimpy getup. Don't go for a run; everybody will fall about laughing when you wobble past, if you get that far.' He raises his hand and she flinches, but he's only reaching into the cabinet. 'Remember when you told me that you felt like doing yourself harm, back in the day when I was the only one you could talk to?'

She's fighting back tears, but she stands firm and faces him as he takes the open razor out of the cabinet, scratching his fingers in his haste.

'Newsflash: nobody cares about you,' he says. 'Here, take this. Do yourself harm now. In fact, do us all a favour and do yourself in. And don't worry, I'll clean up afterwards. Like I always do.'

He holds the razor out towards her and she reaches for it but he pulls it back, teasing her. She tries again and prises it from his fingers, drawing fresh blood. They both wince at the sudden pain as their blood drips onto the floor.

'Oh well,' he says, looking down in mock disappointment. 'I guess I was right about cleaning up.' He looks up and laughs in her face. 'Is that the best you can do? I told you that you were nothing. You can't even slit your wrists properly.'

She slashes the blade across his throat.

Staggering backwards, he clutches uselessly at the bloody gash, staring at her with wide, uncomprehending eyes. Blood spurts against the sink, floor, her. As he slides down the wall the last thing he sees is her staring back at him. Standing tall and still. Calm. Resolved. Accomplished.

Reborn.

She crouches down and leans over the bloody heap that used to be him. Her long ponytail flops over his fixed, startled eyes.

'Who's in control now, *lover*?'

She stands up and walks steadily to the sink. Looks into the mirror at her determined, blood-splattered face. Methodically, she sponges blood off her hair, face, arms, crop-top, torso, shorts and legs.

She looks down again at the mess on the floor and says,

'Looks like I'm the one cleaning up this time.

'Then I'll start running again.'

Stinkface Steffi

Steffi was different. She didn't know why or how she was different but from her first day at school she knew that no one liked her. None of the other kids wanted to sit next to her in class. That wasn't too bad, because she liked this new thing called learning and didn't mind getting on with it on her own. But nobody wanted to play with her either. Playtime was the loneliest time. While everyone else was running about, laughing and making friends, the only child stood in the corner on her own, feeling sad.

Her mum was black and her dad was white, but that didn't make her different: half the kids at school were mixed-race. She was neither fat nor thin, tall nor short, beautiful nor ugly. Her school uniform was as smart as anyone's.

It wasn't too long before she found out. At first, kids turned from her, especially when she opened her mouth. Then they pinched their noses with their fingers, mumbling something that Steffi couldn't hear as they backed away. It was only when her well-meaning teacher told them to say sorry to Steffi for saying something so unkind that Steffi learned what they called her.

Stinkface Steffi.

Her mum always made her wash her face and brush her teeth every morning. Her Afro hair was always clean. So what was stinky about her face? At the end of the school day, a perplexed and hurt Steffi told her mum all about it.

'Why, Mummy?' she sobbed.

Her mum couldn't help but notice the stares and sniggers, not to mention the pinched noses. She glared at the onlookers as she shepherded Steffi away from the school gates to sanctuary at home, where they'd find out what was really wrong.

Steffi's mum was mystified; she couldn't smell anything. Nor could Steffi's dad. There was only one thing to do: they'd have to complain to the school. The teachers needed to understand that they had a *bullying* problem and how *devastating* this was for their daughter. It could give her a *complex* if they didn't *nip it in the bud.* These were her first days at school. They should have been the happiest of her life. But instead she was being bullied into *misery* before her fifth birthday. Steffi overheard some of the conversation between her parents. She didn't understand most of the words, but was sure that she was in some sort of trouble.

The teacher listened sympathetically and without interruption to Steffi's mum's concerns, nodding appropriately when there were pauses, smiling sadly at Steffi, who sat quietly in the corner, scared. The teacher went on to make assurances that bullying was not tolerated in this school and that they took parents' complaints seriously.

Under the circumstances the meeting was going well until Steffi's mum asked if there was anything they could do at home to help their daughter. The teacher bit her lip, took a deep breath, and suggested a visit to the doctor.

'Are you saying there's something wrong with my daughter?'

Steffi didn't understand the sudden outburst. Why was Mum shouting at Miss, who was only trying to help? Was it Steffi's fault? Before she had a chance to ask, Mum dragged her out.

And still nobody had said what was wrong with her.

Sometime after she calmed down, Steffi's mum did take her to the doctor, who, like the teacher, made sympathetic noises as Steffi's mum told him all about the bullying and how worried she and her husband were about their daughter. They were good parents, who loved their daughter and looked after her well. Did Steffi need pills or something?

Pills? All Steffi knew about pills was that you took them when you were sick. But she wasn't sick, so why did her mum think that she needed pills? Pills wouldn't make the other kids like her.

Meanwhile, her mum and the doctor carried on talking about her as if she wasn't there. Steffi lost concentration, picking up only the occasional words. *Allergy. Adverse reaction. Intolerance.* She didn't know what they meant or what it had to do with her. Until she became aware of her mum's angry voice again.

'What do you mean, diet? Are you suggesting there's something wrong with what I feed my own daughter? It's all healthy food!'

Steffi was dragged out again.

Eventually, when her mum calmed down once more, they went to see a *dietitian*. Steffi thought that she knew what this new word meant, because it had the word *diet* in it. This doctor was going to tell her mum how to feed her. So far in her short life, Steffi had seen enough of her mum's angry reactions to guess what was coming next.

However, it so happened that the dietitian and her mum were old friends. While the two women chatted away amicably, Steffi heard those words again: *allergy, reaction, intolerance.* But for a change her mum wasn't getting angry. She and her friend smiled at each other as they looked at recipes, which Steffi's mum took away with her, holding Steffi's hand but not dragging her, for a change.

It was only when they were at the exit that Steffi found out what was actually wrong with her. Something all of the adults knew already, but had been too polite to say. It took a dietitian to finally utter them.

'We'll soon get rid of your *bad breath*, honey.'

It wasn't Steffi's fault. She was only eating what was put on her plate. She didn't know anything about *allergy, reaction or intolerance.*

Steffi would have a new diet, her breath wouldn't smell, she wouldn't be *Stinkface* anymore, and kids would start to like her. After all, despite the bullying, Steffi never bit back, she always tried to *be nice*. Everything would be okay now.

That's not what happened.

Her breath never smelled bad again, but the name stuck. *Stinkface Steffi* forever. All the way through primary school, nobody came round to play with her and nobody invited her to their place.

'Mummy, why doesn't anybody like me? I try to be nice.'

Steffi got used to her own company. She stopped trying to make friends, and kept out of everyone's way as much as possible. Being anonymous was better than being ridiculed. She worked hard at school and played quietly at home, mostly with construction kits; she loved making things and finding out how they worked. Her favourite Christmas presents were a box of cogs and gears and a chemistry set. If the other kids found out about them, they'd probably tease her again for being different, but Steffi lost herself in this new world of discovery. It was her happy place where she could escape from her troubles.

*

Steffi hoped that secondary school would be different, that she could start afresh and make friends at last. However, that unwanted moniker followed her wherever she went. 'That's *Stinkface Steffi*,' her old primary school classmates told the others. Within days, every kid in the school knew, and Steffi's nightmare continued. Physically, Steffi was growing up much like the other girls but emotionally she felt different. Before the end of the first week, she had retreated back into isolation and anonymity.

Nevertheless, after the initial shock and realisation that secondary school would be no kinder than primary school, Steffi gradually developed a sort of resilience. She was so used to being alone that she avoided company without even trying. After a while, most kids ignored her, and her teachers came to know her as the quiet and shy girl in the corner who simply got on with her work. Science and technology, where she learned more and more about how things worked, were her favourites. She had given up on finding the answer to why people didn't like her. She wasn't even sure that an answer existed. But with science and technology, there *was* an answer. A definitive answer, a solution to the problem. Determined, Steffi always arrived at the correct conclusion, and she did it by herself.

Her dad had been quietly supportive throughout the allergy–reaction–intolerance–diet debacle and beyond. One day, he came into his own. He took Steffi along to his rifle club. Which, Steffi understood, was a *big thing*. The club was a bastion of old white men, an anachronism of their former supremacy. But here was *her* dad, her *white* dad, standing up for her and showing the establishment that she had as much right to join their precious club as any of them. She loved him for that.

Surprisingly, after a few grumbles, Steffi was accepted by the rifle club members, which is more than her so-called schoolmates ever did. Those old white men, who had never given the matter much thought before, realised that they had no problem with people other than white males joining the club. Why should they, just because it had always been that way? It was only a tradition, not a very good one, and it was time for it to go. They challenged the taken-for-granted, and grew to admire this quiet girl with the dark skin and black hair that changed its style and direction every time they saw her. They proved to Steffi that they could change and she respected them for that. If only the kids at school could see this, she thought.

Then the rifle club members noticed how much Steffi's shooting was improving. After only a few weeks she was as good as the best of them. *Dead Eye Steffi*, they called her, which was a world away from *Stinkface*. It was the first time that anyone had praised her for being different. Finally, she was *embracing* her differentness. The rifle club became her new sanctuary, where she could lose herself in an activity and forget about *Stinkface Steffi* for a while. She loved feeling the weight of the rifle along her arm. It became part of her as she held it still, breathed deeply, focused through the sights at the target, pulled the trigger.

And hardly ever missed.

Even more than the act of shooting, it was how the rifle worked that captivated her. Fascinated, she took it apart and put it together again. She learned to fix small faults that no one else noticed. As her dad looked on with pride, others approached Steffi respectfully and ask her to service their rifles.

*

Puberty arrived late for Steffi. She understood the science of it, and was complacent about her imminent physical changes. What she didn't anticipate was how those changes would affect her emotions.

Steffi's mum stood her in front of their full-length mirror and said, 'Honey, look at you now.'

Steffi saw someone different from that unhappy girl at the start of primary school who had been neither black nor white, fat nor thin, tall nor short, beautiful nor ugly; who wondered why she wasn't the same as everyone else. Now she saw a tall and slender young woman.

'You're beautiful on the inside and outside,' said her mum. 'You could be a model. You can be anything you want to be.'

What *did* she want to be? A model, parading herself in front of strangers? Exposing her differentness, her aloneness? Both imposed upon her by others and then self-accepted and cultivated for so many years, now to be threatened by crowds?

No, not a model.

Already a riflewoman, what next? A scientist? Yes, that was her dream. Scientists often worked in isolation. She would spend her life discovering new things.

*

Years later, her GCSE options allowed her to study science and technology in greater depth. By now, she knew that she wanted to go to university and follow her dream. It didn't matter that she would do so alone. She had got by without friends so far. Life would be good at last.

However, with her ongoing physical changes came emotional turmoil. Because, after a life in the shadows, her new body was attracting attention. Before quickly averting her gaze and lowering her head, she would notice boys looking at her with something different from derision. So did girls, and one of them actually *spoke* to her. Not being cruel.

Not laughing at her. Not calling her *Stinkface*. Actually being *friendly*.

Her name was Willow, the only other girl in chemistry class, and despite that, one of the cool kids. Mixed race, tall, slender, beautiful. Much like the young woman in Steffi's mirror, except that Willow was confident, assured and *popular*.

'That was a really cool experiment you did there.'

Steffi looked around the room, assuming that Willow was talking to someone else. But when she heard her ask, 'Do you ever experiment with other things?' Steffi did something she had rarely done before. She made eye contact.

'Like what?' she asked.

'Like clothes, makeup, music. Love what you do with your hair, by the way.'

'Thanks.'

'So. Do you?'

'What? Oh, hair, yeah. But the others, not really.'

Steffi was suspicious. She had long ago convinced herself that she could do without friends. Is this what friendliness was like?

Willow smiled and shuffled closer to Steffi. 'Hey, listen to this,' she said, offering one of her earphones to Steffi.

This simple offer sent Steffi into confusion, and something else. Intimacy. Sharing Willow's personal space, connected to her by tangled hair, wire and earphones. Smelling her perfume. Listening. *What a sound.* Thumping drums and bass, crashing guitars, screaming feedback, anger, profanities, impossible noises from the throat.

'What's *this*?' she shouted, not realising that her voice was so loud, and earning her first ever disapproving look from a teacher.

'Shh … It's called *horror punk*. I'll text you the link if you like.'

'Don't have a phone.'

'Babe, you've got a lot to learn. Lemme help you with that.'

And there—sitting in a science lab with her new and only friend, sharing sounds and smells and hair—the next stage of Steffi's education began. Rejection, loneliness, science and technology, rifles. And now … *togetherness*?

Day by day, Steffi, still on her guard, gradually accepted Willow's offers, one by one. Slowly, she was learning to enter Willow's life, and to allow Willow into hers. Two beautiful lives shared. What would people think if they knew about them?

'Who cares about that?' asked Willow. 'Nobody else needs to know.' She scrolled though her smart phone to find one just like it for Steffi. 'Here, write this down and ask your mum and dad to buy you this phone. We'll be able to text and WhatsApp each other. Just you and me. Here, lemme show you how Facebook and Instagram work. And that's only the start, babe.'

'So pleased you've made a friend, honey,' declared her mum when Willow visited.

Sharing clothes, makeup, styling each other's hair. Standing side by side in front of a full-length mirror. Low-heeled, red shoes; bare legs; white skirt billowing out; low-cut red top; immaculately manicured nails, sparkling and artistic; long black hair in braids with multi-coloured beads; dark skin shining; gleaming white teeth; glossy, pink lips; deep brown eyes, dark eyebrows trimmed to perfection, flared eyelashes, black eyeliner curving to a teardrop point.

Flawless.

Identical.

'We could be sisters,' said Steffi, taken aback.

'We *are* sisters,' said her sister.

Finally, the only child was no longer alone. Her first friend. Her only friend. Not only a friend. A sister.

'Remember when I asked you if you ever experimented with other things?' asked Willow.

'Yeah?'

'How about this?'

In the mirror, Steffi saw Willow turn to her, gently push her hair to one side, and kiss her ear, thrust her tongue inside. The sound and feel of part of Willow inside her reverberated, spreading downwards, echoing, infecting. Heart thumping uncontrollably. A warmth in her groin. A quaking in her knees, suddenly weak. She closed her eyes as this new sensation filled her. And then she felt Willow's hands on her face. Opening her eyes, she could no longer see herself in the mirror. Willow's face filled the space in front of hers. Full lips smiling, perfect teeth showing, dark pupils enlarged. It was Steffi's face. And for the only time in the only child's life, she felt a kiss on her lips. And she tasted Willow. And tasted herself.

'But,' said Steffi, 'we're sisters.'

'We're different,' she felt Willow breathe inside her. 'Come with me. We can be *sisters with benefits.*'

Bewitched, Steffi breathed in Willow.

And let herself go.

*

The seasons changed, but Steffi and Willow were constant. They looked alike, walked alike, and after Steffi borrowed Willow's perfume, they smelled alike. They told each other things that no one else would ever know or understand. Willow told Steffi how she was bullied at primary school because of a squint in her eye, which she had to correct by wearing a patch-like mask for months. *Wonky Willow*, they called her, it was a horrible time in her life.

Encouraged, relieved, Steffi confessed to Willow about her own traumatic childhood, revealed her history of *allergy*, *intolerance*, *reaction*, *bad breath*, *Stinkface*. How she always tried to *be nice*. But in return, a life of ridicule. A life without friends. 'Until you, Willow.' It felt so good to let it all pour out.

Willow kissed Steffi tenderly, and listened, understood. Willow gets me, thought Steffi. No one else at school ever gave her a chance.

Willow and Steffi. Steffi and Willow. Each always knowing what the other was thinking, feeling. Always alone together. Exploring each other. Filling themselves with each other. They didn't need anyone else.

Willow sent Steffi photos of them together. Styling each other's hair, applying each other's make-up, dressing and undressing. Intimate moments. Never in public. Private WhatsApp for no one else to see, never on social media for everyone to see.

Steffi hadn't been called *Stinkface* for a long time.

On one of their dressing-up days they delved further into the shadowland of horror punk. Some of the lyrics, those she could make out, resonated with her. The singer rasped and screeched about people hating her, that she was who she was and *fuck everyone else*. Rants about wanting bad things to happen to them. Waste of space. Early grave. Kill them before they kill you. It was escapism, something Steffi knew all about. Willow liked the music, so Steffi liked it too.

She loved Willow, and Willow loved her.

Side by side in front of the mirror. Tight, black leather tops and trousers belted with gargoyles for buckles, jackbooted to the knees, hands gloved with metal knuckles, straightened and spiked black hair topped with military style caps. All black except their faces. Deathly white with red, ghoulish eyes and lips. A horror punk look.

Sinister sisters.

'We can be anything we want to be,' said Willow. 'Let's go to a gig! No one will know who we are. We'll be *sinister sisters doing it for ourselves.*'

Steffi was terrified, but she trusted Willow. So that was okay.

Steffi was finally ready to face the world, even if it would be in disguise. All of her life, since the early realisation that she would never be accepted as one of the crowd, Steffi had tried to blend into the shadows. Be anonymous. Only coming up for air for science and technology experiments. And to shoot. Now she was experimenting again. A new kind of anonymity. Shooting for a different kind of acceptance. Showing everyone who hated her that she was who she was and *fuck them all.*

Willow ordered the tickets online. Willow always organised everything. She would do anything for her *sinister sister.* The date approached and Steffi's nerves and an almost overwhelming insecurity threatened to engulf her. But she wouldn't be alone. She'd never be lonely again. Steffi didn't need to be self-sufficient any more, or hide in the shadows. She had Willow. Willow would make sure she was okay. Willow was everything to her. It was always Willow.

On the night of the gig, she dressed up at home. She and Willow would meet later. As she looked in the mirror at herself dressed exactly as she had been the day that Willow told her she could be anything she wanted to be, she saw Willow looking back at her. Smiling, white teeth shining between red lips in a white face. *You can do this*, *babe,* the image said.

And then she heard the ping of a text.

Willow had Covid.

She couldn't come, but she urged Steffi to go on her own. To show them what she could do. They'd done all the groundwork together. The experiment was so close to its conclusion. She had to see it through to the end. Find the solution. *You can do this, sister.* It was a means to an end. *You can be anything you want to be.*

Nobody would recognise her anyway.

So Steffi went. *Incognito.* Standing in the queue outside the venue, scared inside but disguised outside, she watched herself from the outside. A *white* girl dressed in black for a horror punk gig. Much like most others in the queue. It was a uniform, like at primary school when she *looked* the same as everyone else but was *treated* differently, *felt* different, knew that she *was* different but never found out why. Only now, at last, she *felt the same* as well as *looked the same* as the others.

Even though she was an impostor.

Anonymous.

And with that anonymity came a freedom to lose herself in the adventure. Anticipation as the front of the queue grew closer, the noise from inside booming louder. Jostling for position at the merchandise counter; *must get something for Willow*; texting her updates every five minutes. Standing in her own space as the support band played, her first encounter with live rock music. Bass thudding from the floor, reverberating to her knees, almost settling in her groin before invading her chest. Screaming feedback penetrating her ears.

Then the long wait for the main act. Amidst the multiplying crowd of jam-packed carcasses. Losing her space, finding another, until they all disappeared beneath a mass of black leather, studs, spiked hair, aggression. Elbows pressed into torso; squashed between foreign bodies; smelling their smells; breathing their beer fumes; drinking their sweat; feeling their angst, their anticipation. Waiting, waiting. Background music fading; a rumbling from the crowd; whistling; feet stamping. Another recorded track starting up.

It was only a tease.

A bit boring now, all this waiting. But nobody left, they all waited, and waited. On the outside they're all leather, studs, spikes and hostility, Steffi thought, but on the inside there's patience, loyalty, endurance, seeing it through to the end. Just like me. We're all impostors together.

Background music pausing again, lights dimming, flickering out. Roars from the blackness. And at long last, shadows on the stage. Crowd surging forward, taking Steffi in its wake, before the band they'd all come to see struck their first chord.

Squeezed between a heaving mass of cadavers, Steffi caught a glimpse of the frontwoman, and it was like looking in the mirror again. Tight, black leather tops and trousers belted with gargoyles for buckles, jackbooted to the knees, hands gloved with metal knuckles, straightened and spiked black hair topped with military style cap. All black except her face. Deathly white with red, ghoulish eyes and lips. It could have been her up on that stage, facing down the hostility. It could have been Willow.

'Welcome to my nightmare!' announced the figure on stage. '*Let the horror begin*!'

Crash! Crunch! Scream! Rasp! Rage! Hate me! Love me! Fuck me! Fuck you!

'I! DON'T! CARE!'

Steffi lost herself in the music—became part of the music. Lost in the crowd—part of the crowd. All hostility, aggression, angst—gone. Instead, commonality, togetherness, friendship. *Belonging.*

Outside of the rifle club with its old white men, she had never *belonged* to a group before. Until now. Even though she didn't talk to anyone, she was with them all, sharing the moment. A moment that would never have happened if Willow hadn't come into her life. Willow made her feel welcome, part of something. Accepted, liked, *loved.* This was the New Steffi, and Willow had made it all possible. Willow changed her life. They *belonged* together.

Back on stage, the band's vocalist was singing *to Steffi*. 'You're me and I'm you. People hate us. But I'm beautiful. You're beautiful. *Fuck everyone else!*'

And as she left the stage for the last time:

'I WILL HAVE MY REVENGE!'

Steffi could barely wait to share her revelation with the one person who made it all happen, but she would have to wait until Willow recovered from Covid.

*

Weeks later, texts were pinging back and forth. Willow was recovered, but feeling guilty about not being with the love of her life at her first gig. Could she make it up to Steffi? Could they meet in town, *dressed as horror punks*? Steffi had pulled it off on her own at the gig. Nobody knew her. But nobody would, would they? Nobody who knew her liked horror punk. The next step for Steffi, the next stage in her development, would be to *do it in public*. It would be a laugh. People wouldn't know them as their *alter egos*. It would be the *ultimate experiment*. And they would do it together. *Sinister sisters doing it for themselves*.

On the day of the *ultimate meeting*, Willow sent Steffi a photo of herself in front of the mirror. Tight, black leather top and trousers belted with gargoyles for buckles, jackbooted to the knees, hands gloved with metal knuckles, straightened and spiked black hair topped with military style caps. All black except her face. Deathly white with red, ghoulish eyes and lips.

You can be anything you want to be, babe, texted Willow.

Steffi sent back a photo of herself.

The two photos were a perfect match.

Just like Willow and Steffi.

We're ready, they texted.

*

Steffi walks *incognito* along the street. All in black except her deathly white face. Not strutting, but with trepidation, anxiety, paranoia. Is everyone looking at her because of her clothes or because *they know who she is?* But she can't allow herself to think like that, to *be* like that. She's not the sad, downtrodden, lonely Steffi any longer. She's the New Steffi. Bold, confident, proud to be herself, to be different and, at the same time, to *belong*. She can be anything she wants to be. All the same, she's scared, but it'll be okay. Willow will be round the next corner and everything'll be fine. Willow always makes everything okay.

She turns the corner and there's the café where they've agreed to meet outside.

Willow's not there.

Never mind, she thinks. I'm early, she'll be here soon, everything's going to be fine.

There's a boy from school waiting outside. She knows who he is and she knows he knows who she is, usually. But he won't recognise her in disguise.

Or will he?

'Well, look who it isn't.' he says. 'Hi, Steffi, *Honey*.'

'But—'

'But what? How do I know it's you? Black face, white face, I'd recognise that *Stinkface* anywhere.'

'Wha—'

'What am *I* doing here? You're about to find out, *babe*.' And he winks at her as his gaze shifts towards the café door.

Then the *real* horror begins.

Low-heeled red shoes; bare legs; white skirt billowing out; low-cut red top; immaculately manicured nails, sparkling and artistic; long black hair in braids with multi-coloured beads; dark skin shining; gleaming white teeth; glossy, pink lips; deep brown eyes, dark eyebrows trimmed to perfection, flared eyelashes, black eyeliner curving to a teardrop point.

Willow smiles at Steffi, walks casually over to the boy, cups his face in her hands and kisses him hard, swallowing him up as though she's dying of thirst. One leg hooked around his backside, she thrusts her body into a twisted embrace. When eventually she comes up for air she faces Steffi, sniffs and says, 'Hi, *babe*. Nice costume.'

Frozen in time, Steffi will remember this moment and wonder how she managed to stay on her feet. Swaying, knees trembling, looseness in her bowels. She's vaguely aware of others joining the scene, pointing phone cameras at her as she struggles to come to terms with this devastating change to the new way of life that she's learned to embrace. Piece by piece, the solution to the cruel puzzle is revealed.

'Where—'

'Where what? Where's *my* costume?' taunts Willow. 'In the bin.'

'But—'

'But? Oh, *the photo*? That's the one we took ages ago. You remember that time, don't you, *Sister*?'

'But the gig, you—'

'Got the tickets, yeah, I got the tickets, *babe*. Oh, you thought I was actually coming? I wouldn't be seen dead with those zombie losers. Horror punk? I hate it. You're the horror, *honey*. It's worth ten times the price of the tickets to laugh at your stupid face right now. I mean, *look* at you. Black face, white face, whatever, you're a *disgrace to your race*.'

A large crowd has gathered, hanging onto Willow's every utterance. At first muffled sniggers, then giggles, then …

HA-HA-HA

'But you—'

'Had Covid?' Willow coughed. 'Fuck all wrong with me, *honey*. There's never been anything wrong with my eyes either, except when I have to look at you, *sister*. Never had to wear no stupid mask neither. But *you* should, to hide your stupid fucking *Stinkface*.'

HA-HA-HA-HA-HA

'But we—'

'Had sex? *Who cares about that?* You wanna know how it felt? It made me sick. I was gagging. I think I've got an *allergy* or something. Listen to me, I'm coughing now,

I think I'm gonna retch any second. Yeah, an *intolerance*, that's it. An *adverse reaction* to *you*, *Stinkface Steffi*.'

HA-HA-HA-HA-HA-HA-HA

'Why—'

'Why *Stinkface*? Cause every time you open your fucking mouth, s*hit* pours out,' she spluttered.

HA-HA-HA-HA-HA-HA-HA-HA-HA-HA

'You and your shitty science experiments and your shitty face and your fucking shitty body. Think you look like me, do you? You'll never be like me. I'm *me* and you're *you*, *Stinkface Steffi.*'

HA-HA-HA-HA-HA-HA-HA-HA-HA-HA-HA-HA-HA

'But *why*?'

'Why did I do it? Because it was an *experiment*. Because you made it easy for me. Always had to *be nice*, didn't you? Couldn't see past the shit in front of your eyes, could you? You fell for everything, you stupid *Stinkface Sister*. I did it because I can. I can do anything I want. Be anything I want to be. People *love* me cause I do what I want and tell it how it is. Nobody loves you, *honey*. People *hate* you. *You* can't change, *sister*. You know why, *babe*? Cause you'll *never* change. You'll always be poor, lonely, Little Miss No Mates, *Stinkface Steffi.*'

HA-HA-HA-HA-HA-HA-HA-HA-HA-HA-HA-HA-HA-HA-HA-HA

Everything about the last months of Steffi's life, everything about Willow, has been a lie. Willow had made her feel part of something, Willow welcomed her into her life, Willow was interested in her for who she really is, Willow loved her.

All lies.

HA-HA-HA-HA-HA-HA-HA-HA-HA-HA-HA-HA-HA-HA-HA-HA-HA-HA-HA

*

Steffi never remembered exactly what happened next.

How she staggered from the scene of her ultimate humiliation, while Willow spewed out her toxic vitriol, bent over double, wheezing, hacking.

How Steffi ran the gauntlet of ridicule, tears streaming down her chalked white face, rivers of shame.

How she escaped to the sanctuary of home. Which was no escape at all. Because the humiliation, hurt, devastation, betrayal refused to leave her.

That's when she discovered the *evil* in the world of social media. She didn't even know that other people could find her on her phone. It had always been her and Willow's private place. After only minutes of watching her humiliation on screen—*nobody loves you* HA-HA-HA-HA *everybody hates you* HA-HA-HA-HA-HA *who cares about that?* HA-HA-HA-HA-HA-HA *black face, white face, disgrace to your race* HA-HA-HA-HA-HA-HA-HA-HA *Sister, babe, honey, STINKFACE* HA-HA-HA-HA-HA-HA-HA-HA-HA-HA—she took herself off Facebook and all the rest of that shit, and stamped her phone into pieces, destroying all traces of her brief venture into so-called happiness. So false. So many lies. How had she fallen for them all? How had she been so gullible? Willow had plotted Steffi's downfall for months. What sort of *horror* was she? But which of the two *sinister sisters* was the real *horror*? Because Willow was Steffi and Steffi was Willow. Or used to be. Who did Steffi see in the mirror now that her delusions had been shattered?

She smashed the mirror.

Steffi spent the next week in bed. Shapeless pyjamas, blotched face, lank hair. Occasionally venturing downstairs to the sofa.

'What's wrong, honey?' asked her mum. And Steffi's tears gushed again. *Honey*—her mum might as well have called her *babe* or *sister* or *Stinkface*, they were all the same to her now. She'd never hear any of them again without reliving her worst nightmare. *The horror.* Without picturing the hateful face of Willow, *Beauty Fiend.* Beautiful on the outside, ugly, twisted evil on the inside. *Twisted sister.*

At least her mum had the sensitivity not to mention Willow's name as she engulfed Steffi in her arms and muttered soothing noises.

Her dad looked on quietly and worriedly.

The next day he took her back to the rifle club.

Where the old white men welcomed her back.

Where, with the comforting weight of the weapon, she rediscovered her focus. Sight. Aim. Squeeze the trigger. Fire. Hit the target.

Willow did have Covid after all. Long Covid. And a long absence from school, which made Steffi feel safe enough to go back. Without Willow it was easier to avoid the other bullies. There were still sniggers and taunts but Steffi ignored them, outwardly anyway, and eventually the bullies got bored. The goading reappeared when Willow returned, but even the *Nightmare Queen* eventually succumbed to boredom and moved on to a new target.

*

Years passed. Steffi's A levels were a welcome distraction from her lingering shame. She conducted further experiments in science and technology, learning even more about how things worked, making new discoveries, being noticed for the right reasons, by teachers anyway. At home she cooked and styled her hair with her mum, went shooting with her dad, listened to horror punk on her own. A place at university assured, she looked forward to a fresh start, the *real* horror left behind.

She didn't really believe that.

The nightmare never left her, even after all these years.

To consign it to the past, she couldn't just wait for it to disappear.

It never would.

She'd have to do something about it.

Make something happen.

But what?

She stood in front of her still-taped-up mirror and stared into her eyes.

Not Willow's eyes.

Steffi's eyes.

I need to make it all disappear, she decided to herself. The shame, the hate, the *horror*.

But how?

And then it came to her.

The school prom was coming up soon.

There was going to be a prom queen.

Willow.

Who would be on stage for all to see.

A target.

Steffi had to be there to have her revenge. But not as herself. She would go *incognito* again. Back in the shadowlands. Her previous disguise hadn't fooled anyone, but she knew more about how things worked now, how to construct them.

Two words on the prom poster showed her the way.

Masks essential.

An illustration made it clear that they didn't mean the boring masks they wore during the extremes of Covid. It was going to be the formal wear of masked balls from Georgian times.

How bizarre, but it would serve Steffi's purpose.

Steffi created her prom gown at home. It was all red, cascading to the floor, high-necked, full sleeves, black gloves. It had to be a loose fit for padding, so that she could disguise her slender frame. She would look frumpy but *who cares about that*? Her hair would be dyed white with black streaks and piled up above her head. She would have loved to adorn her white mask with multi-coloured beads, but it had to be plain for her scheme to work. It needed to cover her whole face, not only the top half like the old Georgian masks. She wouldn't be in the hall for long, but she couldn't run the risk of anyone recognising her this time. And this mask would have a special feature; she knew how to make that work too.

There would be a few more crucial preparations. There were things she needed. Things that she couldn't possibly sneak past security on the night. She knew where to get them, and where to hide them in the shadows of the hall. Before the *ultimate party*.

Victim no longer, she said to herself:

I will have my revenge!

*

Steffi walks *incognito* along the street. All in red except her black gloves, white hair and white mask. Not quite strutting, but with purpose. She can do this. She's not the sad, downtrodden, lonely Steffi any longer. She's the New Steffi. Bold, confident, proud to be herself, to be different, *not* to belong to the gathering crowd of excited school leavers. Glamorous girls in gorgeous gowns tumbling out of limos. Boys dressed in formal suits like James Bond and trying to act suave. Knocking back the welcome glasses of prosecco, laughing and high-fiving with their friends as they lift up their masks to reveal their identity. If they see a frumpy girl in a baggy red dress they quickly ignore her. Nobody knows who she is. So far, it's working. As Steffi knew it would.

Standing in the queue outside the venue—confident inside, disguised outside—she watches herself from the outside. A dowdy girl trying to dress up for the prom and not quite pulling it off. Different from the others in the queue. Not like at primary school when she *looked* the same as everyone else but was *treated* differently, *felt* different, knew that she *was* different but never found out why. Now at last she is her own person.

Even though it's not really her.

Even though she's

An impostor.

Anonymous.

Again.

She passes security without incident, as she knew she would. It's only a forged ticket: child's play. Not like the final pieces of the jigsaw, hidden in the shadows.

No jostling for position, no elbows pressed into torso, no squashing between bodies, no breathing their prosecco-fumes, drinking their sweat, smelling their smells. But lurking in the shadows on the edge. Locating the final pieces of the puzzle soon to be solved at long last. Waiting, waiting … to see it through to the end.

The music fades, the auditorium lights dim and flicker out. Shafts of startling luminosity strike the stage, highlighting the microphone stand and a glimmering trophy. The prom queen's trophy. From the blackness—whistling, stamping feet, mumbling, building to a roar. And at long last, the moment they have all been waiting for.

Waiting in the wings, hidden in the blackness, Steffi watches the prom queen take to the stage. Red dress, black gloves, red lips, white hair piled above her head. The frontwoman removes her white mask adorned with multi-coloured beads, and Steffi sees herself. Dark face shining; gleaming white teeth; glossy, pink lips; deep brown eyes, dark eyebrows trimmed to perfection, flared eyelashes, black eyeliner curving to a teardrop point.

She's in the mirror again. Self-assured, glowing, beautiful.

Cheers from the crowd, but also some boos. What's this? Little Miss Popular isn't so popular after all? Steffi's been out of touch, but she doesn't have time to think about that. She has work to do.

Willow, in the startling light, faces down the hostility and starts her acceptance speech, mouth up close against the microphone. All smiles and giggles and radiance as words gush from her mouth.

In the gloomy shadows, finger poised on the penultimate piece of the jigsaw, Steffi remembers:

'I can do anything I want to do. Be anything I want to be. People *love* me cause I do what I want and tell it how it is. Nobody loves you, *honey*. People *hate* you. *You* can't change, *sister*. You know why, *babe*? Cause you'll *never* change. You'll always be poor, lonely, Little Miss No Mates, *Stinkface Steffi*.'

She squeezes the trigger.

And the microphone explodes, spewing a fountain of *shit* at Willow's face, into her mouth, up her nose, in her ears.

The dark crowd falls silent. Then Steffi hears muttering, stifled giggles. And then:

HA-HA-HA-HA-HA-HA-HA-HA-HA-HA-HA-HA-HA-HA-HA-HA-HA-HA-HA

Willow does look pretty funny. Red lips pulled back in a grimace, perfect white teeth stained with shit. Tongue stuck out, trying to escape from her cesspit of a mouth. White eyes staring in *horror* out of a chaos of excrement. Ice cream hair streaked with chocolate-coloured rivulets. Red arms hanging stiffly by her sides, helpless as the brown filth drips off her chin, down her beautiful red ballgown. A splattered queen, tormented, disgraced, humiliated. A grotesque parody of her former beauty.

HA-HA-HA-HA-HA-HA-HA-HA-HA-HA-HA-HA-HA-HA-HA-HA-HA-HA-HA

Back in the shadows, Steffi watches her *alter ego* fall from grace.

'Who's the *Stinkface* now, *sister*?'

Two *sinister sisters*, once again connected by wires. Not the short-lived kind, intimately linking them via horror punk, a lifetime ago. But by a missing link, long and hidden, from microphone to trigger.

Dead Eye Steffi isn't laughing.

'Think that's funny?' she asks the dark horde and *everyone* who ever called her *Stinkface*. 'I haven't even got started yet.

'*Welcome to my nightmare.*

'*LET THE HORROR BEGIN.*'

She squeezes another trigger, and completes the jigsaw. It's the *final solution.*

The crowd will never remember exactly what happens next in the darkness. At first they're aware only of the putrid stink of shit. Some kind of *gas* seeping out of the walls, the ceiling, the floorboards. Engulfing them, penetrating their noses and mouths, stinging their eyes. Wheezing, coughing, retching, hacking. Hands covering mouths, fingers pinching noses or trying to squeeze stinging pain from eyes. Jostling, pushing, panicking, rushing, stumbling, tripping, colliding, falling, staggering to find an escape, any escape. *This is not an exit.* Wrong place, too dark. Fumbling, shoving others aside, surging, blindly seeking the sanctuary of the night air. Nothing else matters.

Willow stands on stage, exposed in the blinding light. A pungent, barely human tower of shit. Quivering. Swaying. Arms still frozen at her sides as if she can't bear to touch any part of her own stinking torso. Even her eyes are frozen, oblivious to the stinging fumes. Face locked, grimaced. Disgust, shock, horror, helplessness. In their rush to escape, nobody goes to the prom queen's aid. No one even looks at her. As the seething panic below subsides, Willow is left alone, rigid in the glare. Deserted.

No one sees the girl in the baggy red dress and white mask crawl out of the shadows and creep around the side of the stage towards the back exit.

No one except Willow, who in the corner of a mud-splattered eye sees a shapeless form in red shuffling in the shadows. Torso still frozen, Willow's neck distorts and creaks horribly as she slowly twists her head to the side. Through the murk she struggles to focus on a white face gleaming in the blackness.

Steffi peers between the slits in her mask, adapted to protect her from the noxious fumes. She sees Willow staring at her plaintively, white eyes piercing the brown sludge. Pleading.

Help me.

Prolonged exposure to the toxicity will cause irreparable damage to eyes, nose, throat, lungs. Steffi knows this; she created the concoction. She knows that the heaving crowd outside will recover; they escaped in time.

But not Willow.

Steffi, silhouetted against the gloom, pauses. There on the stage, her nemesis, her betrayer, her enemy, the personification of a lifetime of misery. A solitary and forlorn figure, numb, frigid. A few minutes longer and Willow's body will begin to shut down. Hours, perhaps days or weeks later, but inevitably, Willow will die. And Steffi will have her revenge.

A pair of eyes behind a plain white mask squints at a stage mirror, and sees an identical pair of eyes, staring out of the decay of a brown, mutilated mask.

The eyes lock.

Steffi crosses the stage, embraces Willow's stained, stinking, ruined body. Drags her off into the shadows, through the rear exit and into the night. Where she leaves Willow awakening from her stupor, wheezing, hacking, spewing.

*

The morning headlines screamed:

PANICKED EXODUS FROM MASKED BALL

MASS EXPOSURE TO POISONOUS GAS

PROM QUEEN DOUSED IN HUMAN EXCREMENT

RIFLEMAN APPREHENDED

VICTIMS DESCRIBE—

'Whoa!' Steffi said to herself. '*What* rifleman?'

She read on: *toxic fumes empty building before a single shot fired … network of wires and piping discovered … school leavers saved from potential massacre … rifle club report theft … prom queen in intensive care … other casualties recovering well …*

It was months before the truth came out. The so-called rifleman was another victim of Willow's vitriol. The same boy who had been outside the café years ago, waiting for Steffi's horror to begin. Now he was living his own nightmare. Sobbing, he revealed how his lover had teased him, reeled him in, netted him and then threw him back, humiliated and broken. His would have been the *ultimate* revenge, but a shower of shit and a crappy cloud of noxious gas got in his way. No, he didn't know anything about any wires or piping. Driven blindly towards destruction, he didn't even know how to fire a rifle.

No one ever suspected the shy, reclusive girl with the occasionally strange taste in clothes. Who, unwittingly, had prevented a far worse revenge than the one she had concocted with such meticulosity and achieved with such perfection.

But this quiet, reserved young woman went on to university in another town, where she achieved her longed-for fresh start. She became the star science student, breaking new grounds in discovery. She dressed up again for horror punk gigs and made new friends, who, captivated by her striking appearance, invited her to perform in their bands. Steffi politely declined because she had other interests too. She joined the university shooting club and became a national students' champion. Elected club captain, she helped others achieve their goals, earning their unreserved respect. Everyone admired her commitment and individuality.

She never whitened her face again.

No longer the impostor, she was her own self at last, and everyone loved her for it.

Willow survived the effects of her prolonged exposure to toxicity, but never recovered from her humiliation. During a long stay in hospital, no one came to visit. She was eventually allowed home, and lived in an isolated, semi-vegetative state, broken only by nightmares, when she screamed about zombies, shit, *horror.*

She never found out who rescued her from certain death on the night of her demise.

Steffi left university with a doctorate, and became a scientist of global and international acclaim. One day, when she returned to her home town, she saw Willow on the other side of the street, hanging onto her mum for support, shuffling unsteadily in shapeless, colourless clothes. Hunched body, lank hair, blotched face with sunken eyes.

Eyes that met Steffi's across the street.

Steffi slowly turned her head.

Away from the mirror.

And walked on, never to see her *sinister sister* again.

Steffi was a survivor.

Not only surviving.

Thriving.

Her *alter ego* long dead.

No one would ever hear again of *Stinkface Steffi.*

EAT_SLEEP_RUN_REPEAT_

Early promise at club junior section
Fun running
Should try other events too
Not listening
Just want to run
EAT_SLEEP_RUN_REPEAT_

Early success
School Sports winner
Area Sports winner
Always hungry
Eat more
Run more
Not listening
EAT_SLEEP_RUN_REPEAT_

County Schools sprint champion
Want to run further
Not listening
EAT_SLEEP_RUN_REPEAT_

National schools middle-distance champion
Want to run faster for longer
Need to train more
Not listening
EAT_SLEEP_RUN_REPEAT_

Run half-marathon
Good time for age but want faster
Legs hurt for days afterwards
No pain no gain
Need to train more often and for longer
Not listening
EAT_SLEEP_RUN_REPEAT_

Leave school and go to university
No more home cooking
Eat when hungry
Can eat anything and everything when training hard
Not listening
EAT_SLEEP_RUN_REPEAT_

No more club coaching
Doesn't matter
Not listening anyway
Just run with the squad
And run extra miles solo
EAT_SLEEP_RUN_REPEAT_

Want to run a marathon
Need to run even more miles
Legs hurt *before* run
Don't take any notice
Don't listen
Just keep running
EAT_SLEEP_RUN_REPEAT_

Not skinny enough
Have to be skinny to win
Not listening
Eat less
EAT_SLEEP_RUN_REPEAT_

Still not skinny enough
Fat fat fat
Not listening
Eat even less
EAT_SLEEP_RUN_REPEAT_
Marathon Day
Get to twenty miles
Legs in agony
Feel faint
Can't finish
Injured
Can't run
Need to keep fit for the next marathon
Cycle instead
Not listening
EAT_SLEEP_CYCLE_REPEAT_

Cycling burns fewer calories than running
Fat fat *fat*
Need to cycle more
Eat hardly anything
Not listening
SLEEP_CYCLE_REPEAT_

Can’t sleep
CYCLE_REPEAT_

Almost asleep in the saddle
Fall off
CRASH

Hospital
On drip then liquids then solids
EAT_SLEEP_ REPEAT_

Discharged
Not listening
Still injured
Worse after the crash
Still can't run
Now can't cycle either
Fat *fat* FAT
No training = *even fatter*
Eat less again
Not listening
SLEEP_ REPEAT_

Still can't cycle or run
Still fat
Not eating
Not listening
Must keep fit for next marathon
Try swimming
SLEEP_SWIM_REPEAT_

Can't sleep again
SWIM_REPEAT_

In pool changing rooms
COLLAPSE

Hospital again
Back on drip then liquids then solids
EAT_SLEEP_ REPEAT_

Discharged again
Not listening
Fat *fat* FATTER THAN EVER
Not eating
Need to get back in the pool
Not listening
SLEEP_ SWIM_ REPEAT_

Can't sleep again
Need to keep training
Not mixing
Not listening
Not speaking
Have to run that next marathon
SWIM_ REPEAT_

Lose consciousness in the water
No one notices
NO REPEAT_
DELETE.

If you enjoyed these stories, you may also like:

No Cross-Country for Old Men – A Story of Loss, Resilience and Running
by Brian Gardner

David Sharpe: Enigma on Track – Wild Child to World Champion
by Brian Gardner and David Sharpe

Printed in Great Britain
by Amazon

28581655R00148